HYDE

I : Jack

Written by C. T. York

ISBN 978-1-0688329-1-8 (Hardcover)
ISBN 978-1-0688329-2-5 (Paperback)
ISBN 978-1-0688329-0-1 (E-Book)

Hyde I : Jack is currently only available via Amazon marketplace in hardcover, paperback and ebook formats. New formats and translations may be made available in the future.

For business inquiries contact wttg.ct@gmail.com Merchandise is available at store.streamelements.com/wttg_ct with discounts available for twitch subscribers.

For updates on the future of Hyde, follow me for free on twitch at WttG_CT where we enjoy gaming, game creation and a mental health positive environment/safespace for all. I hope you will be a part of my community in all its mediums. Welcome to the Grid my friends.
www.twitch.tv/wttg_ct

First Edition: May 2024

Special thanks to the prodigal son on Twitch for the tremendous support and assistance during the launch of this project. Wishing you all the best. Check out this wonderful human being on Twitch at www.twitch.tv/prodigal_sonttv.

I want to extend a special thanks to G (Sicah). You have been the brother I never had, and in a world where family can sometimes disappoint, I am grateful to have found a true friend in you. Through thick and thin, I value our friendship immensely.

Lastly, a heartfelt thank you to JJ. Life may throw challenges your way, but remember you have the strength to overcome them and shape your future. Don't let anyone else define who you are or what you can achieve. The power to determine your destiny lies within you

Chapter 1   1
Chapter 2   7
Chapter 3   16
Chapter 4   28
Chapter 5   33
Chapter 6   41
Chapter 7   49
Chapter 8   55
Chapter 9   62
Chapter 10   66
Chapter 11   72
Chapter 12   80
Chapter 13   88
Chapter 14   96
Chapter 15   106
Chapter 16   110
Chapter 17   115
Chapter 18   122
Chapter 19   132
Chapter 20   142
Chapter 21   145
Chapter 22   148
Chapter 23   162
Chapter 24   168
Chapter 25   180
Chapter 26   186
Chapter 27   195
Epilogue   198

shoulder. The alley, flanked by imposing red brick buildings, becomes an eerie channel for his escape.

The fog, an ethereal presence, hangs low, weaving through the air, wrapping around every nook and cranny like a phantom's embrace. Streetlights cast feeble glows, futile against the thick mist. A quick look backward reveals merging low fog and encroaching darkness, a macabre dance resembling the hand of a reaper reaching out to pull him into the abyss. His response is a visceral howl, echoing through the alley, an attempt to drown out the encroaching feeling of dread.

Ducking into an alcove amidst the hushed stillness, a wave of relief washes over him, and he breathes a whispered affirmation, "I think I made it out." Rising cautiously, he casts a final glance around, each step forward accompanied by a growing ominous rumble reverberating through the ground. His eyes widen in terror, and a scream tears from his throat as an unfathomable force seizes him, subjecting him to a brutal and unrelenting onslaught.

In the ensuing turmoil, he transforms into a marionette in the violent puppetry of an unseen malevolence. The force lunges towards him unforgivingly, tearing through the air and sending him hurtling in unpredictable trajectories. Limbs flail wildly, manipulated by an inscrutable power that renders him a mere pawn—a puppet tossed about in the clutches of incomprehensible malevolence. Each impact becomes a savage punctuation mark, a harrowing collision of raw power and desperate struggle.

The creature, an architect of chaos, persists in its assault with relentless vigour, akin to the ferocity of a canine with a new toy. He is thrown about, a series

of brutal exclamation marks in a narrative of

aggression. His world becomes a dizzying whirlwind

as the creature, gripping him like a dog shaking its

prize vigorously, lashes him around with abandon.

The assailant grants no respite; its actions are more

sensed than observed—a formidable force of upheaval.

In this violent ballet, the man's body bears the weight

of an assault by an inscrutable adversary, crafting a

vivid tableau of suffering and pandemonium.

His lifeless body, swiftly revolving in the air,

descends rapidly to the ground. With a resounding

crash and a wet splat, the broken form lands on the

roof of a car in the neighbouring lot. The impact

forces the roof to collapse, shattering the windows

outward and sending fragments of glass scattering

wildly around the wreckage. The body hangs limp and

lifeless, blood dripping slowly from the mutilated corpse.

Despair settles as what once was a man now lies as mere meat, resting in tatters—his form reduced to ribbons, fit only for scavengers' delight. The car emits a hushed creak, groaning beneath the unexpected rooftop addition, while the wind, akin to a ghostly maestro, conducts a dissonant symphony through the broken structure. Parked in the desolate lot, the vehicle stands as a haunting testament to the chaotic events that unfold in the adjacent alley, casting a forlorn silhouette against the backdrop of the looming, darkened building.

Fragments of moonlight sift through the clutter, darkness, and mist. Then, with a sudden stir, the dormant building offers a subtle sign of life, as if rousing from slumber. A lone neon light hums to life, gradually illuminating the surrounding darkness. In a mesmerizing crescendo, the neon intensifies, casting a vivid spectrum of luminescent colours across the parking lot and the building's façade. The once-muted surroundings now dance with an ethereal vibrancy.

As the sign fully hums to life, it gradually unveils a mysterious symbol—an animalistic silhouette paired with two words. In a climax of luminescence and shadow, the proclamation of words on the sign emerges—ominous yet unmistakable:

The Jackal.

Chapter 2

The midday sun reached its zenith, warmly embracing the bustling lot. Its rays kissed the pavement, igniting a subtle dance of heat in the air. Vehicles marked with the acronym ICIS, representing the Illinois Crime Investigative Services, are placed strategically like a vigilant bulwark. Their metallic surfaces absorbed the sun's warmth, radiating it across the asphalt. Yellow crime bands crisscrossed the parking lot, forming a protective shield amidst orchestrated chaos. Their vibrant hue stood out against the concrete backdrop, signalling caution to all who entered.

In the heart of the bustling lot, a scene of gruesome carnage unfolded, a visceral display of violence and horror that seared itself into the minds of all who beheld it. Strewn across the unforgiving pavement were fragments of shattered glass, glinting malevolently in the harsh light of day, each shard a jagged testament to the brutality of the event. Pools of thick, coagulating blood pooled beneath the wreckage, mingling with chunks of torn flesh and sinew, their sickly scent hanging heavy in the air, assaulting the senses of those unfortunate enough to draw near. Amidst the grisly tableau, twisted shards of metal protruded grotesquely, sharp edges stained crimson with the lifeblood of the fallen, a chilling reminder of the destructive force that had torn through the scene with merciless abandon.

A cyber orange Ford Mustang glided to a halt just outside the perimeter, its tires whispering a muted protest against the pavement. The golden driver's door slowly opened, revealing Megan Briar as she stepped out. With a purposeful stride, she emerged, her fishtail-braided blonde hair neatly tied to the side. Her emerald eyes were hidden behind her aviator sunglasses' gleaming golden rims and dark frames. She surveyed the grim scene presented to her. In her tailored ensemble, she exuded professionalism at 5'7", wearing a dark navy double-pocket regent blazer, matching cameron pants, a black long-sleeve v-neck top, and sleek Clark's Emily 2 Dove Pump shoes in black. Seizing a bag from the back seat, she took a deep breath and went to the crime scene.

"Hello, Megan! I had no idea you were assigned to this case," the coroner greeted, rising from his work to welcome her.

"Yes, Aldo, unfortunately, I am. I wish I had been informed earlier; I would've skipped breakfast," she replied, walking toward him with a nod.

Already on-site, Aldo Brandt cut a figure of composed authority. Donned in the practical ensemble of blue scrubs, a sleek black lab coat, and the necessary protective accoutrements, he radiated professionalism. Short brown hair neatly framed his face, underscoring a defined jawline that spoke to his wealth of experience and unwavering determination. Standing at 5'11", he embodied a readiness for the challenges of fieldwork that garnered respect from those around him.

Megan Briar and Aldo Brandt were standouts during their high school years, both earning the title of valedictorian for their academic excellence. Their journey from valedictorians to excelling in their respective fields showcased exceptional abilities and unwavering commitment, laying the groundwork for their collaboration in the challenging world of crime investigation.

"So, what do you have at the moment?" Megan asked, her eyes methodically scanning the scene as she walked cautiously toward the wreckage. Retrieving a pair of gloves from her bag with a deliberate rhythm, she accompanied the action with a small pointer. Despite her experience, her mind involuntarily flickered back to past cases, sensing an unsettling difference in this one from the others. She had seen violence but never this gruesome.

"The victim is unidentified; there's no wallet yet. The wounds on him seem to be post-mortem, likely sustained from landing on the car parked here. However, these..." Aldo carefully moved forward, directing Megan's attention to other wounds on the body. "These appear to be perimortem, suggesting an attack by some animal before being thrown here."

"They do resemble large claw marks," Megan said, her brow furrowing in concern. "But, Aldo, this is downtown. I find it hard to believe that anything this substantial would go unnoticed."

In the silent recesses of her thoughts, Megan contemplated the unusual nature of the scene. The distant hum of traffic provided an eerie counterpoint to her introspection. Meticulously observing the body, she made detailed notes in her notebook with a practiced hand. Her commitment to note-taking had proven crucial in solving cases before, and she believed these observations might hold significance in the future.

As Aldo carefully displayed the body, Megan leaned in for a closer look. "Were there any traces of animals in the wounds or around the scene?" she inquired, her mind already at work to piece together the puzzling aspects of the case.

Aldo scratched his head thoughtfully. "It's puzzling. Based on our initial inspection, here's my take: I plan to conduct a more thorough examination in the morgue, but the injuries seem consistent with those caused by an animal. If it's a blade, evidence might be visible from a deeper perspective. What surprised me even more were the findings from the technicians who examined the scene. Despite the scattered pieces of glass and metal from the car, as well as bits of flesh and blood from the body, there's no other evidence around us."

Surveying her surroundings, frustration etched across her face at the news, Megan's gaze fixed on the looming building. Its shadow casts a cool contrast to the heated crime scene. "What information do we have about that?"

"The building?"

"Yes."

Aldo looked up, wiping the sweat from his forehead. "Absolutely nothing. I thought it was abandoned, but that sign looks brand new. Quite odd."

"I agree," she said, pointing to the door and the strategically placed cameras on the walls. "They also have cameras. Has anyone checked them?"

A nearby forensic tech acknowledged the conversation and shook her head.

Megan stepped towards the door. "Aldo, if you find anything else, take note and tell me before you leave."

"Will do, Megs," said Aldo, looking down and returning to work.

"Not at work!" She huffed at his casual nature on the job while walking to the two large doors of the building.

Chapter 3

As she approached, her gaze lifted to the dormant neon sign, its finely crafted glass emitting an eerie glint in the daylight, casting a ghostly shadow on the wall. The figure of a mysterious feral creature loomed on the sign, its features obscured in the dimness. Beneath it, the words "The Jackal" were etched in bold lettering, seeming to pulse with otherworldly energy as the sign twisted into shape. The name almost reverberated in the stillness of the air, sending a shiver down her spine. 'Maybe you're involved,' she breathed, her voice barely more than a whisper, as she attempted the doors. They were locked. Knocking forcefully, she called out, the sound reverberating through the quiet street, 'ICIS, is anyone inside?'

Silence.

She realized she needed to identify the building's owner, so Megan glanced at her notebook, making notes. The scratch of her pen against the paper punctuated the silence.

Suddenly, a small pot light inside flickered to life, casting an eerie glow that danced with the shadows behind the door. Accompanied by a resounding clunk from the door lock, startling her and causing her to take a step back. Bewildered, she scrutinized the door, searching for any sign of movement on the other side. With trembling hands, she extended her hand and pulled the handles. The hefty doors groaned open with a loud creak, filling the air with a musty scent that tickled her nose. Stepping cautiously inside, Megan felt uncertainty linger like a heavy fog. She drew her weapon, a Smith & Wesson

Performance Center M&P 2.0, its cool metal

reassuring against her skin.

"ICIS, I need to speak with the building's

owner."

Only the haunting whistle from the wind

blowing against the building and the encompassing

darkness greeted her.

"There are cameras outside, and we require

copies of the surveillance footage for an ongoing

investigation. I request your cooperation. If necessary,

I will seek a court order to compel your compliance.

Could you please step out and turn on the lights?"

The dimly lit interior responded, gradually

illuminating small pot lights that beckoned Megan

deeper into the building. With practiced precision, she

steadily held her trusty M&P 2.0 drawn. The lights

paused, revealing an open room with a raised platform.

Megan scanned her surroundings vigilantly. A light twinkled above her, momentarily dazzling her as she turned her attention towards it. She noticed a silhouette on the upper floor. Looking around for a way above, Megan saw stairs in a side alcove, the steps outlined by faint lights that followed the contours of each step upwards. She ascended cautiously toward the stairs, repeating, "I'm Agent Briar from ICIS. Please identify yourself."

Upon reaching the top step, she observed the shadows around her and on the lower floor. Peering into the darkness, Megan discovered a spacious round seating area. In that second, the movement below captured her attention. Glancing towards the open floor, the lights abruptly extinguished. "Fuck," she murmured.

In the darkness near her, two resounding knocks against the floor echoed.

The dim lights flickered back to life as Megan turned toward the source of the noise. At the center of the seating area sat a man leaning forward. He was clad in a sleek black suit tailored to perfection, accentuating his slender frame. A matching black vest adorned his torso, adding a touch of sophistication to his ensemble. Beneath the vest, a crisp white shirt peeked out, its fabric immaculately pressed. He clutched a cane and was crowned by a tall top hat. His attire exuded old-world charm, meticulously accentuated by the thoughtful selection of each element.

Megan aimed her weapon at him. "Identify yourself!"

"There is a more pleasant way to ask that," an accented voice calmly emanated from under the hat.

"I'm..."

"Agent Briar of ICIS, and you want my security footage."

A bit caught off guard, she kept her weapon at the ready. "Yes, an incident took place outside."

"If you want to talk, show me the courtesy of putting down your firearm."

Thinking momentarily, she holstered her M&P 2.0, opting for a more diplomatic approach.

"You appear frightened by the dark," he said calmly.

She glared at him. "No, I…"

"The unknown, perhaps?"

"Well, maybe, but I…"

"Darkness is unknown. It conceals that which the light would reveal."

"Stop interrupting me."

"As a matter of fact, you were interrupting me. This is my place of work, and you came to speak to me, weapon in hand."

Megan closed her eyes for a moment; *calm down, Megan, just a day-to-day asshole.* She thought, urging herself to calm down. "Look, I have protocols to follow. I identified myself; you had not responded and chose to sit in the dark instead. I drew my weapon for my security."

"Unfortunate."

"What's unfortunate?"

"That you require such vulgarities in the name of safety, it's unfortunate."

Megan closed her eyes again, and she re-centered herself. "Let me start over correctly."

"You may."

"My name is Special Agent Briar; I'm with ICIS and need to ask you a few questions related to the ongoing case I'm handling."

"You're free to ask your questions, officer," the man calmly responded.

Megan shot him a piercing glance. *What's with this guy?* "By the time you arrived, did you see the body outside?"

"No."

"What about the car? Is that owned by you?"

"No."

"What time did you get here?"

"I've been here all night. My office is in the back, and I occasionally sleep there to avoid overworking."

"Have you heard anything strange outside since yesterday at this moment?"

"No, I have not."

This guy irritated her, not to mention his unsettling demeanour. He sat like a statue, his hat casting shadows over his face, giving off a creepy vibe. She could tell he stared at her through the unsettling darkness, though.

"What's your name, and what is this business exactly?"

"This is the Jackal. The place is a bar, a nightclub. And the name... the name is Jack, Jack Blakely."

Once again, Megan retrieved her notebook and began jotting down notes.

"Jack, Jackal, is that wordplay?"

"No." She sensed a change in his tone, but he remained still as he responded to her.

"Oh. Do you possess a permit, and is the establishment currently operational?"

"We've been open for years. I had to step away for a spell, which led us to conduct some renovations. Despite the recent lack of clientele, the building has never become obsolete."

"I see. Regarding the surveillance cameras..."

"I regret to inform you that they are currently out of order. Unfortunately, contractors working on renovations mistakenly cut some vital wires, resulting in the system being down for the past month."

She eyed him with distrust. *How can a man afford to sustain his business without keeping it open? And, despite being attentive in other areas, why would he let something like surveillance fall short for a month?* Megan cautiously extended her hand with a business card she withdrew from her pocket.

"If there are any further questions, we'll be in touch."

Jack remained motionless by her action.

"You may see yourself out."

Megan awkwardly retracted her hand and returned the business card to its home, curtsying as she turned away. Descending the stairs towards the exit, the encounter with Jack occupied her thoughts. Why did she just curtsy? She felt like a fool, yet the peculiar aura of that man lingered in her mind. Megan struggled to trust him and the veracity of his statements.

Chapter 4

After hearing the door shut and lock behind Agent Briar, Jack strolled through the premises, each step sending a soft creak through the floorboards underfoot. Jack cuts a commanding figure, his stature standing at 5'11". His short, dark brown hair is concealed beneath the brim of a distinguished top hat, tipped low as he liked it. Clad in an impeccably tailored old-style suit and matching vest, his muscular frame is evident even beneath the layers of fabric. An aura of authority and confidence surrounds him, accentuated by the subtle gleam in his piercing eyes and the faint hint of a knowing smirk playing at the corners of his lips.

The polished wooden cane in his hand taps rhythmically against the floor with every step. Using his free hand, he runs his fingers along the polished surfaces of every piece of furniture, savouring the scent of aged wood and leather in the air. From the intricate carvings on the chairs to the faded photographs on the walls, he scrutinizes every detail precisely. The room is enveloped in the rich aroma of aged scotch and whiskey, mingling with the subtle scent of dust and old memories.

As he reached the bar, Jack abruptly halted, his eyebrow arching as he peered towards the entrance to the kitchen. Faint echoes of clinking bottles and soft rustling created a delicate symphony, adding depth to the quiet surroundings.

A man emerges from the entrance, his voice barely above a whisper, filled with apprehension and deference. "Should we be concerned?"

Jack's calm yet authoritative voice resonates through the room. "No. Law enforcement's actions won't impede us from handling this situation properly." He tilts his head slightly, his intense gaze seeming to pierce through the man's soul.

"Briar. She is..."

"I'm aware. And that's an ordeal she should never experience if I can prevent it." Jack's concern seeps into his voice, a rare glimpse into his emotions.

"The victim outside..."

Jack turns slowly, meeting the man's gaze with unwavering intensity. "You understand the plan. Ensure his family is duly compensated. They are not burdened; they have the means to move forward comfortably."

The man hesitates, uncertainty flickering in his eyes.

"That was a message for us, wasn't it?" His tone shifts, revealing the concern beneath the surface.

"It was." Jack's response is clipped, and his determination is evident.

"And our response?"

"Monitor the situation. I'll address it... personally, when the time comes," Jack's cryptic words were characteristic of his reserved nature. He always prefers to keep information close, revealing it only when necessary. This usually kept him in a better position, while others missed uniquely positioned pawns he could reposition later.

"Of course, my lord." The man's voice is filled with reverence.

"Sentinel. Avoid that name. There must not be any room for error. Moving forward, you know the proper way to address me." Jack's words cut through the air with precision.

"Yes, sir." The man lowered his head slowly.

With a graceful step backward, the man fades into the shadows, leaving behind a palpable silence. The tension hangs heavy in the air, unspoken words lingering between them.

Jack despised being left messages, viewing them as futile attempts to control him. Those responsible should recognize the imprudence of assuming control. It's not anyone's place to dictate his actions except his own. If Jack was compelled to retaliate, it would be a decision they'd come to regret deeply.

Chapter 5

Megan sat at her desk, her fingers tapping rhythmically on her notebook as she meticulously reviewed the evidence gathered from the scene. The faint aroma of freshly brewed coffee permeated the air, mingling with the sharp tang of ink from her pen as she scribbled notes in the margins.

The car, registered under a corporate entity, presented a mysterious disconnect, seemingly vanishing into thin air with no tangible connections. Megan clicked through the photographs and files in the digital folders before her on the screen; she scrutinized the documents meticulously, searching for any clue that might unravel the mystery.

As Aldo pointed out, the fragments comprised glass and metal remnants from both the vehicle and the victim. Despite this, the forensic analysis turned up nothing significant—a vexing dead end. Megan furrowed her brow in frustration, the tension in her shoulders palpable as she sifted through the files of scattered documents on the work server.

Feeling exasperated, Megan got lost in her thoughts; *how could holding physical evidence yield no answers and only lead to more perplexing questions?* The soft hum of the overhead fluorescent lights filled the room, casting a sterile glow over the cluttered workspaces as Megan ran her hands through her hair, trying to calm her racing thoughts.

She meticulously sifted through every detail related to the bar—The Jackal. There were no signs of foul play and no evidence of any suspicious activity. Everything appeared to be up to date. Megan navigated the intricate web of alphabet agencies, reaching the highest echelons to gather comprehensive information. The unsettling aspect was the immaculate cleanliness of the business. The faint scent of disinfectant hung in the air, mingling with the aroma of coffee, paper and printer ink as Megan pored over the files before her, searching for any hint of wrongdoing.

Interrupting her thoughts, music wafted through her surroundings. The soft strains of a familiar melody filled the room, soothing Megan's frayed nerves as she glanced at her phone and pressed the answer button. "Hello."

"You seem frustrated, my darling," a voice responded. Megan's heart skipped a beat at the sound of Devlin's voice. A warm rush of affection washed over her as she leaned back in her chair, a small smile tugging at the corners of her lips.

Devlin Alastor, Megan's steadfast partner of two years, possessed an intuitive understanding of her needs. Standing 6'o" with short dark brown hair, he exuded a calming presence that enveloped Megan like a warm embrace. His experience navigating the intricate workings of the legal system, acquired during his tenure at the District Attorney's office, imbued him with a unique insight into handling challenging situations. Devlin's knack for discerning the right words to soothe Megan's troubled mind and guide her focus back to the task at hand made him an invaluable source of support amidst the chaos of her demanding caseload.

"Devlin. No, I... maybe I am." Megan's voice was soft, tinged with exhaustion as she ran a hand through her hair, the tension in her shoulders easing slightly at the sound of Devlin's voice over the phone.

"In that case, what's the challenge? Is it a tough case?" Devlin inquired, his voice filled with concern.

"Yes, but you know I'm not allowed to talk about it," Megan responded, her voice tinged with frustration as she pushed the papers and keyboard aside, focusing her attention on the comforting sound of Devlin's voice.

"You'll pull through, I'm sure." Devlin's confident voice was reassuring in the midst of Megan's turmoil.

"Maybe you can be of some help." Megan's voice was hopeful, and there was a faint glimmer of anticipation as she considered the possibility of Devlin's assistance.

"Anything." Devlin's voice was warm, a soft chuckle escaping him as he offered his unwavering support.

"You visit bars and clubs for work, treating clients. Right?" Megan's voice was hesitant, a note of uncertainty creeping into her tone as she considered Devlin's expertise.

"Yes. Why do you need me to help you get... undercover?" Devlin's voice was teasing, and he had a playful glint in his eye as he imagined the possibilities.

"No, stop tempting me on the job. Have you been to the Jackal before?" Megan's voice was playful, a small smile tugging at the corners of her lips as she imagined Devlin's reaction.

"No, should I try it or steer clear of it?" Devlin's voice was curious, and there was a hint of intrigue in his tone as he considered Megan's question.

"No, nothing like that. I couldn't find much and wondered what it looked like from a customer's perspective." Megan's voice was thoughtful, a faint frown creasing her brow as she considered the implications of her words.

"Shall I take you?" Devlin's voice was eager, a warm rush of excitement coursing through him as he imagined the possibility of exploring the Jackal with Megan by his side.

"Maybe if one day I find my social life. Unfortunately, that case will remain unanswered." Megan's voice was wistful, a faint sigh escaping her as she considered the demands of her job.

"I'll hold you to that. It's not work-related. Can I help with that?" Devlin's voice was gentle and reassuring amid Megan's crisis as he offered his unwavering support.

"No, go to work," Megan replied, laughing lightly, before hanging up. Putting the phone in her pocket, she checked her notes and headed to the ICIS war room.

Chapter 6

"Mortimer Stithulf, a Caucasian male, 38 years old, unmarried, stood tall at 6'2" and weighed 237 pounds," Aldo read aloud, clicking through the photos projected on the screen. "The autopsy indicates the cause of death to be from the deep wounds throughout the body. This likely caused him to bleed to death. The strikes perforated his internal organs, causing impact fractures and internal lacerations. The time of death is estimated to be between 2 and 4 a.m. It was instantaneous, leaving no traces behind."

The ICIS war room stood as one of the agency's remarkable features, contributing to its status as one of the best state-level investigative agencies. A fully digital environment, it facilitated swift briefings for agents, allowing them to dismantle and reassemble tools in a matter of seconds for the next team's use.

Case details were stored digitally and redundantly saved by clerks who generated hard copies for filing purposes. While various teams contributed to the case, only leads or superiors had the authority to remove uploaded assets, leaving a clear trail aiding legal teams in evidence processing.

In attendance were Aldo, the meticulous medical examiner; Erika Collette, the special agent in charge of this local ICIS office; and Team Two, composed of two highly skilled agents—Agent Salma Karida, known as Kari, and Agent Osmond Truman, known as Oz.

As the special agent in charge of ICIS in this region of Illinois, Erika Collette, standing at a confident 5'8", exuded a radiant deep-brown complexion—a testament to the exquisite blend of her French-African heritage. Raven-black hair framed her face with a regal touch, amplifying the aura of strength and confidence she radiated. A warm, engaging smile graced her features, harmonizing with expressive eyes that unveiled depth and sincerity. More than a leader, Erika was a pillar of support, carrying herself with innate sophistication; each action resonated with a quiet grace that spoke volumes about her character.

Kari, a dedicated young woman of Arabic descent, emphasized her commitment to a structured and organized demeanour with the grace of her neatly pulled-back black hair. Standing at a striking 5'3", her poised posture radiated readiness for any challenge. Having already carved a path as a trailblazer within the agency, she exhibited a sharp mind and impressive physical capabilities. A pervasive aura of sophistication and capability surrounded her, making

Kari a formidable presence in the agency's ranks.

At a commanding 6'3", Oz captured attention

with his lean and tall physique. A seasoned former

British marksman, he initially caught ICIS's eye

during his tenure as an arson inspector. His seamless

transition into the agency was fueled by a

commendable track record marked by a remarkable

closure success rate. Possessing striking blue eyes and

short blonde hair that complemented a well-defined

jawline and high cheekbones, Oz showcased classic

features contributing to his charismatic presence.

Together, they formed Megan's leading team in the

field.

"I understand both Oz and I arrived late at the

crime scene, but Aldo, was there really no forensic

evidence?" Kari inquired, flipping through her tablet notes.

"Not a single damn piece of trace," Aldo replied with evident frustration. "If I were to attempt to craft a perfect murder scene, envisioning something like this wouldn't even cross my mind. It's perplexing to create such chaos while leaving virtually no forensic trail behind. Our technicians scoured every inch and found no signs of hair, cuts, fibres, or fluids. It's as if the unsub wore a hazmat suit, ensuring no shred of evidence was left behind. Frankly, it felt like I was penning a science fiction novel in my report. I apologize, chief," he added, reflecting his discontent. Megan could sense Aldo's frustration, knowing him as someone who never returned empty-handed due to his meticulous work ethic she had witnessed on multiple occasions.

"Aldo, while I am troubled by the fact that this case is puzzling you, don't hold in the frustration and be mad at yourself. Your role is to present the facts, as you always do, and rely on your team to unearth the answers," reassured Erika, a stern leader known for her firm yet supportive demeanour; she didn't waste her words. Megan admired her for these qualities.

"Any leads from the crowd or local canvas?" Megan shifted her focus to Oz.

"I coordinated the canvassing with the agents. There were reports of late-night disturbances, and a few claimed to have spotted the body the next morning. However, nothing tangible or conclusive emerged during the ETD," Oz reported. His efficiency at work was evident, but the lack of evidence on the case unsettled him.

Megan changed the screen to a picture of the Jackal and Jack. "Well, my search hasn't yielded much either. The property, the Jackal, is registered under Jack Blakely's name. Despite its thriving nightclub and bar history, no one seems to know anything beyond the fact that it's been closed for a long time. Strangely, all the necessary permits are still in order. Maintaining such assets in this manner is a financial burden, yet everything remains up to date. If Blakely is behind this, how is he funding it all? I couldn't dig up any information on him. He's so squeaky clean it makes me feel like I need a shower. No one is that pristine." The team slumped visibly, a wave of defeat washing over them.

"I agree; it's rare to find someone so immaculate. Is there any prior or background information on Mr. Blakely?" Erika inquired, glancing

at Megan.

48

"You could always question the source," a voice

from the doorway interrupted, startling everyone. The

ICIS agents turned to see that the man on the screen

had intruded into their war room.

Chapter 7

"What the hell is this about? The mayor, Erika, and two of her superiors?" Megan's voice was barely above a whisper, her gaze fixed on the doorway leading to Erika's office. They were locked in conversation with Jack Blakely, the closest thing to a suspect in their investigation. Despite her simmering frustration, Megan's face showed no signs of anger. What bothered her most was no one in the office seemed angry, adding an eerie tension to the encounter.

Jack casually tipped his hat as he exited Erika's office, his movements fluid and graceful. His sharp eyes scanned the bustling activity of the ICIS teams below, taking in every detail with a keen observation. Jack exuded an unmistakable aura of refinement, dressed in a dark ruby red vest accented by an antique pocket watch chain and crowned with his top hat. He cut a striking figure with his polished cane in hand, simultaneously blending in and standing out amidst the office's organized chaos. His eyes stopped at Megan as he slowly descended the steps towards her.

"Hello, Ms. Briar," Jack greeted, his tone smooth and composed.

"It's Agent Briar. What exactly are you doing here?" Megan's irritation was palpable as she tapped her foot impatiently, Kari and Oz watching closely from their nearby desks.

"Agent Briar, then. I'm here to offer my assistance," Jack replied with a slow, deliberate bow.

"Assistance? You're currently under suspicion in an ongoing investigation!"

Jack met Megan's gaze with a faint frown. "If you find me guilty, feel free to arrest me on the spot, no questions asked, no changes to our agreement." He raised his wrists in a mock surrender.

Feeling increasingly frustrated, Megan shot back, "Of course, I'll arrest you! Wait, What agreement are you talking about?" As Megan paused, caught off guard, Erika approached to address the agents.

"Ladies and gentlemen, as you're aware, we're faced with a complex case that presents more questions than answers. Mr. Blakely has generously offered ICIS financial assistance, ensuring our operations will remain robust and keeping us at the forefront of investigative services," Erika announced, gesturing toward Jack.

Jack removed his hat and addressed the room. "Indeed, my contribution isn't entirely altruistic. I've invested in ICIS to ensure you have state-of-the-art investigation tools. As discussed with your bosses, I'll be advised of the expenditures to ensure I am satisfied that funds are allocated appropriately, considering the percentages I've specified for different areas. With my personal interest in this case, I hope these enhancements expedite your work, allowing me to proceed with my plans to reopen. May justice for the victim be swiftly achieved with the assistance of your talented agents."

Jack bowed graciously as the room erupted in applause, but Megan's skepticism remained. Jack turned his attention back to Megan. "That is the agreement. The money is legitimate. If I'm found guilty, your agency retains the donation. But I think if we do this, we should talk. I should be questioned properly to alleviate your distrust of me."

Erika signalled for Megan to join her. Megan gave Jack a suspicious look as she walked towards Erika. "Yes, Chief?"

"The mayor contacted my superiors. He has asked on Jack's behalf if Jack could offer his services." Erika looked towards the agents working and Jack, who was now talking with the mayor.

"Services? What services? He also just bribed us!"

"No, my superiors know and understand that Jack is a person of interest, and they agreed that the funding is safe and not a bribe. The donation has no conditions apart from being divided among all divisions, with some receiving more than others. Jack has offered his records voluntarily, including financial information. In terms of his services, Jack has worked in the past for a well-known private investigator. The mayor vouched for Jack's investigative talents personally." Erika was harsh in her words and looked back at Megan. "Jack has also offered to cooperate fully if we find grounds to arrest him."

"This doesn't sit right with me."

"It's above our pay grade. Question Jack thoroughly, then let's get to work," Erika replied firmly, her gaze shifting back to Jack. Jack looked back and smiled, standing there with calculated confidence as if the entire situation were part of a twisted game.

Chapter 8

Jack sits comfortably at the table, his top hat resting beside him, his polished cane leaning against the chair, and his tailored jacket impeccably draped over the back. He takes a leisurely sip from a water bottle, condensation trickling down its cool surface. "What would you like to know?" he asks, calm and composed.

Megan and Kari sit across from Jack, Megan studying him intently. Behind the one-way mirror, Erika and Oz observe the interrogation, their eyes focused on the interaction. "Your money. Where does it come from?" Megan probes, her tone sharp with suspicion.

"It's hard to explain," Jack begins, his gaze meeting Megan's unwaveringly. "In essence, I come

from old money. Yet, I choose to live modestly,
preferring not to flaunt my wealth. This donation
doesn't dent my financial standing, and the interest it
earns remains unaffected. I believe in the gradual
redistribution of wealth. I give little by little, but the
world has to support itself."

"You just donated two billion dollars and claim
it doesn't affect your interest," Megan counters, her
skepticism evident.

"Yes, it's from generational wealth,
well-guarded for ages. Banks don't readily divulge
information about their wealthiest clients, and
companies may compile lists of the world's richest
individuals. They could conduct investigations or use
information in the public domain. However, if one
avoids drawing attention, their name won't appear. As
far as public records go, I'm hardly noteworthy; in

fact, I probably appear to be living beyond my means and in the red."

Megan finds his explanation peculiar but makes a mental note to investigate further. "Your club has been closed for some time," she continues, shifting the conversation.

"It's a family legacy," Jack explains. "I've been discreetly renovating to minimize disruption to the neighbours. We're in the process of reopening. I've managed similar establishments before, even one in New York recently that we chose to close before coming here."

"Closed?" Megan probes.

"Yes, temporarily. The property remains mine and will be well-maintained in my absence, but I prefer a hands-on management approach."

As Jack speaks, Megan notices the confident air about him. Her research and the information she found followed what he was saying. Maintaining his own businesses has helped him cut costs and ensure that no one gets greedy or has sticky fingers. She couldn't shake the feeling that she had. Megan hadn't heard of anyone with that level of money. It seems unfathomable, either ill-gotten or, like Jack said, inherited from a distant past.

Kari leans in, whispering to Megan. This was sometimes a successful strategy to unsettle Jack or other interrogation subjects. "When was the last time you visited Illinois?" Kari asks, standing up and circling him like a predator, looking for a hole in his armour.

"When I was younger," Jack responds calmly. "Thanks to my vast financial resources, I travelled often, I would find an interest or hobby to indulge in, and if I got bored, I would move on to something new."

Kari presses further, hoping to catch Jack off guard. "If we ran your prints through the databases, what would we find?"

"I don't anticipate anything significant," Jack replies evenly. "I have regular problems but abide by the law; I always have."

Kari's gaze sharpens, smirking slyly. "According to your standards or the actual laws?"

"I'm sorry? Are you asking me whether I consider myself beyond the law?"

Kari stands up straight, looking down at Jack. "The wealthy act as if things don't apply to them; they do as they please."

Jack meets her gaze squarely. "No, rules exist for a reason. When you come from a family like mine, making an international fool of yourself invites trouble from undesirable groups. An unlimited source of wealth for fueling a terrorist campaign or launching a new war. Maintaining a low profile is very essential in my position. Is there anything else you'd like to know?" Jack looked between Kari and Megan, doubtful they were satisfied.

Megan opens a file, placing photos of the victim on the table before Jack. The atmosphere shifts as she and Kari switch positions. "Are you familiar with this man in the photo?" Megan asks, her tone firm.

Jack studied the photos carefully before shaking his head. "No, I haven't met him personally. Contractors frequented the site, but I didn't interact with each and every one of them. He may be, but I don't remember seeing him myself." Jack's body language revealed nothing.

Megan exchanges a glance with Kari and then looks at the two-way mirror. Without solid evidence, there's little they can do. They had nothing, and it was useless to pound a point without a nail.

Erika steps away from the glass. "Let him go," she instructs.

Oz sighs and taps the glass, signalling the end of the interrogation.

Chapter 9

"I understand your skepticism. The mayor is seeking Jack's assistance. I don't want him left alone or handling evidence while he's involved in this case. You can take this as an opportunity to observe him closely, you know, 'keep your friends close and your enemies closer.'" Erika gazed out of her office window, overseeing the ICIS teams. The distant hum of city traffic echoed through the glass, mingling with the muffled chatter of agents in the bullpen below.

"Yes, ma'am," replied Megan, seated at the desk. She felt a surge of frustration as the case took a challenging turn, and now her suspect was being brought in to assist. The harsh glare of the overhead lights cast shadows across the cluttered desk, adding to Megan's sense of unease.

"What's your next move?"

"We'll follow up on the victim. We have a local address to investigate." Megan's fingers tapped lightly on the desk, a nervous habit she couldn't shake. The faint scent of coffee wafted from a nearby mug, mingling with the sterile aroma of the office.

"With our limited options, proceed with that plan. Take Mr. Blakely and observe for any slips from him or anyone else." Erika took her seat, the leather creaking softly beneath her. "You have your orders."

Megan rose and headed towards the door. "Yes, ma'am." The cool metal handle of the door felt reassuring in her grip as she stepped into the bullpen.

Exiting the chief's office, Megan strode towards team two. The dull thud of footsteps echoed in the corridor, punctuated by the occasional murmur of conversation. She stopped before the team, waiting by the elevators' seating area.

"The verdict?" inquired Oz as he stood up.

"We have to collaborate with Mr. Blakely's support. Additionally, we need to head to Mr. Stithulf's residence, the victim." Megan moved between Oz and Kari to address Jack. He rose as she approached, the soft rustle of fabric accompanying his movement. "You're on thin ice. The mayor requested that we accommodate your involvement. You won't be alone, won't handle evidence, and won't carry a gun. Consider it a courtesy."

Jack nodded slightly, tipping his hat.

"Understood, Agent Briar. Where are we headed?"

"To investigate our only lead." Megan led the way to the elevators, her footsteps dulled by the open space around them.

Under Megan's lead, team two approached the metal doors as they opened. Megan couldn't shake the eerie sensation trailing them. Jack followed closely his sinister smile concealed in the shadows of his hat, his cane rhythmically tapping with each step. The faint scent of rain lingered in the air as they exited the building, a harbinger of the storm brewing on the horizon.

Chapter 10

In the eerie aura of an abandoned warehouse strewn with useless debris, a haunting shadow casts its presence in the diminishing light of sunset. The vast, desolate space permits the wind to weave through the open door frames and shattered windows, crafting an unsettling breeze. Gabriel Raymond, Jack's sentinel, emerges into the scene. He is a tall and authoritative man, hiding his inhuman abilities. His shaved head and strong jawline enhance his already imposing demeanour. Draped in a flowing, long black coat, he completes his ensemble with light gold wide rectangle rimless tinted sunglasses, sleek black dress slacks, and durable Dr. Martens black boots.

After the conversation with Jack at the Jackal, Gabriel was tasked with using his abilities to track down whatever being was causing these issues. While

Jack was unique and walked between the mortal and supernatural worlds, Gabriel preferred staying in the shadows as Jack's protector.

Coming to an abrupt halt, Gabriel exhales with a tangible gravity, shaking his head. Retrieving his phone from his pocket, he initiates a call. The distant echoes of his footsteps blend with the faint rustle of windblown debris.

"Sir, I regret to inform you that it has claimed another victim. I'll leave the information in the usual place. I apologize for the delay in executing my assignment. Moreover, this individual was the driver of the truck. It's unmistakably a message directed at you." Gabriel walked around the space, taking a mental inventory as he talked.

"Additionally, as per your request, I've taken the liberty to establish an account for the other. I will adhere to the same protocol for this one." Gabriel's voice resonates through the desolate space, mingling with the soft groans of shifting metal.

Gabriel swiftly terminates the call, conducting a thorough sweep of the immediate vicinity. Retrieving another phone from his pocket, he meticulously cleans its surface. He dials 911, a strategic move, and initiates a timed call using a specialized phone app. The distant hum of nearby traffic blends with the phone's quiet clicks.

Emerging slowly from the warehouse, Gabriel lifts his gaze to assess his surroundings. The roof is within reach, and he assumes a poised stance. Kneeling a tiny bit, he applies gentle pressure against the ground, resembling a coiled spring. The resulting action defies human limits, propelling him into the air and gracefully onto the rooftop. His ascent is accompanied by the faint rustle of his coat in the wind.

From this elevated vantage point, Gabriel meticulously scans the rooftop until he identifies a small crack in the infrastructure. Advancing purposefully, he inserts the cheap burner phone into the confined space. His movements are fluid, almost dance-like, as he works with practiced precision.

On numerous occasions, he flawlessly executed this meticulous routine. The covert nature of his work demanded absolute privacy, compelling him to systematically cleanse the scene, eradicating any potential clues that could expose sensitive information to mortals. The elusive being he pursued left no trace, leading to the decision to officially report the incident. A well-coordinated plan unfolded: an application that places a call to authorities and simulates distress and subsequent destruction of the phone upon the

confirmation of the location by the police trace.

Concealed at this strategic vantage point, the

hidden-phone afforded him ample time to ensure

thorough obliteration before discovery. It would be

incinerated meticulously if it stumbled upon, leaving

no discernible traces or forensic evidence.

Rising from his task, Gabriel gracefully moved

to the roof's edge. The height, sufficient to break the

legs of anyone unfortunate enough to stumble off, had

no impact on Gabriel as he defied the laws of physics,

making a three-point landing with unrivalled grace.

His coat floated momentarily, stirred by the displaced

air from the extraordinary descent. A final, cautious

sweep of his surroundings affirmed his satisfaction

with the completed mission. Silently, Gabriel

proceeded down the alley, going to the car parked

several lots away. The faint scent of exhaust mingled

with the cool night air as he disappeared, as he had

arrived... from the shadows.

Chapter 11

As Megan steps out of the SUV, the cool breeze tousles her hair, carrying the faint scent of gasoline from the nearby street. Glancing at her notes, she absorbs the details about Mortimer Stithulf. He was never married, lived alone, and worked as a courier for a delivery company. She could feel the solitude of his existence; it felt palpable in the air. Anticipation builds as they await the landlord's arrival, who will soon provide access to the apartment for further investigation.

Jack emerges from the back seat, adjusting his vest with a slight rustle of fabric before deftly sliding on a pair of sunglasses, shielding his eyes from the setting sun's glare.

"So, you mentioned he worked for a delivery firm during the ride, correct?" Jack's voice cuts through the quiet, and Kari joins him as she rounds the vehicle.

"That's correct," Kari affirms, her footsteps crunching on the gravel.

"Any knowledge of which one he worked for?" Jack looked at the others.

Oz, engrossed in his tablet, taps away, checking the information. "Not yet; other agents are looking into it, but we might find the answer while we are here."

"Jack, I'd like to remind you that your role is to observe. If you come across something substantial, you will inform me. Otherwise, be seen but not heard," Megan's voice carries authority as she returns to her notes, phone pressed to her ear as she calls the landlord.

"That's rude. But I will oblige. You are, however, ignoring my talents." Everyone ignores Jack's comment as the team moves toward the building without him. Feeling like he is being watched, Jack looks around in the direction he feels the eyes and sees a figure discreetly observing them from behind a parked vehicle. He grinned sinisterly and mentally noted the stranger before following the others inside.

Jack walked down the building hallway toward the unit mentioned in their earlier conversation. As he approached, he noticed the door to the apartment was already open. Stepping inside, he observed that it looked surprisingly clean for a bachelor's dwelling, with piles of magazines neatly arranged on the nearby table. The dishes in the sink were unwashed but appeared to be no more than two nights' worth. The faint scent of lemon-scented cleaner lingered in the air, adding a subtle freshness. Jack's footsteps echoed softly on the polished floor as he explored the space further. In the background, he could hear the warm and comforting voice of the elderly female landlord as she conversed with the team.

"He was quiet, and he paid everything on time—there was never a complaint from him or against him from other tenants," the landlady said. Her words paint a picture of a peaceful tenant.

She looks like she managed property to earn income during her twilight years. It's doubtful she knows anything substantial. Jack thought to himself as he listened in to the conversation.

Oz nods attentively, the scratch of his pen on paper punctuating the conversation. "When he moved in, did you require an employment record?" he asked, looking up from his notes.

"No, I have tenants here who live with support. Not everyone has a job. As long as they don't cause issues and pay on time, I leave them alone," she responded.

Jack's attention shifts from the conversation to the recent mail on the table. He slips on a pair of gloves and carefully sifts through the pile. Stopping on a pamphlet he deems strange, he removes it from the pile. Flipping it over, he reveals a cryptic message: 'Join the light, Let him in,' marked with a strange symbol. Jack recognizes the symbol as a bastardization of something he's seen before, a strange sun symbol. He slips his phone from his pocket and takes quick pictures of it. Glancing around to ensure no one is watching, Jack slips the pamphlet into his pocket. As Megan steps closer, gently intervening, her gloved hand covering the mail, he returns to his search through the pile.

"Observant without touching," Megan whispers, glaring at his immediate disobedience. She takes the mail from his hands, but he manages to grab one envelope, the crinkle of paper barely audible. He holds it up to show her the logo in the corner of the envelope, reading 'Milk & Honey Transportation.' Jack looks at Megan as she snatches it away from him.

"Temper, temper. That's a company I use. They are in charge of my alcohol deliveries. You asked me to inform you of anything substantial, correct?" Jack's voice is low, meant for Megan's ears only.

Megan looks at Jack momentarily, unable to read him or his intentions.

Megan turned her attention to the letter, opened the envelope and scanned it. It was a letter reminding Mr. Stithulf to use his vacation days before they expired. She took note of the company to remember to contact them later. She looked back at Jack, speaking in a hushed tone, "Good work, now do as we told you. There is a chain of command. You are not allowed to touch potential evidence. Don't touch anything; we will talk after."

Meanwhile, the room buzzed with activity as Oz and Kari continued their investigation. Megan glanced over to assess their progress. Oz remained engaged in questioning the landlady, his tone devoid of suspicion, while Kari supervised the other agents as they meticulously cataloged and inventoried the victims' belongings. As for Jack, he stood suspiciously near the door, prompting a sense of unease in Megan. She couldn't pinpoint why Jack irked her but couldn't shake the feeling. To compound matters, she harboured a hunch that Jack was again involved—this thread she intended to unravel.

Megan's phone rings, the sudden interruption breaking her out of her thoughts. "Briar. Where? We're on the way." With a swift glance at her team, she issues a directive to the agents in the room. "You need to finish here' then she turns to team two, "we need to go. There's been another incident." her commanding voice resounding with authority. Team Two exits the apartment with a sense of purpose, their footsteps echoing in the hallway as they hurry to their next destination.

Chapter 12

In the expansive warehouse, Aldo was encircled by forensic investigators meticulously scrutinizing the scene. In his familiar on-site field attire, he ensured comfort and protection while he pursued a thorough examination. Despite their concerted efforts, a void of trace evidence persisted, and another lifeless body augmented the already sombre tableau. The doors and walls bore slashes yet offered no clues for identification. The enigma seemed more like a mini Mecha Godzilla was more responsible than anything the current investigation could make sense of.

As Megan and her team entered the warehouse, chemicals lingered in the air, mingling with the faint aroma of dust and old machinery. Jack trailed behind, his footsteps echoing against the cement floor.

"Sorry, Megs. It's the same – nothing forensic to speak of yet," Aldo reported to Megan, a notable hint of frustration evident as he shook his head.

"It's okay, Aldo. Do you have any insights on the victim?" Megan inquired, her voice echoing slightly in the cavernous space.

"He drove the truck," the voice behind them said. Turning around, Megan and Aldo fixed their gaze on Jack. "This is someone I did know. He worked for Milk & Honey and was a driver for them. He had a family." Jack's gaze shifted downward, and his tone darkened.

Megan shifted her focus to Aldo, inquiring, "Time of death?"

"Early estimate puts the window between 2 - 4 p.m. today," Aldo responded, his words punctuated by the low hum of agents working around them.

Megan mentally retraced the events of the day: Jack's arrival at 1 p.m. and the current time at 10 p.m. It seemed implausible for him to be involved in the crime. However, a lingering suspicion persisted.

"What's the story with the 911 call this time?" Megan asked, her brow furrowing in concentration.

"Dispatch received a call with what sounded like laboured breathing. The dispatcher sent both an ambulance and the police in response to the call. Officers entered first, followed by the medics. They reported back, and that's when we were notified; it might be related. Officers are still on the scene, but the medics had to leave for another call. I did manage to secure the 911 call recording." Aldo gestured towards a flash drive and a laptop set up nearby.

Walking over, Megan inserted the flash drive and launched it into the ICIS dispatcher program, which analyzes the recorded data dispatcher networks collect and compile. A city map, wave file, and dispatcher log materialized on the screen. With a press of a button, she set the playback into motion.

"911, what is your emergency?" The dispatcher's voice crackled through the speakers, accompanied by the faint buzz of electronic equipment.

The second wave file showed signs of life, though faint. There was no verbal response, only laboured breathing and slight rustling.

"Hello, are you all right?" Megan was visibly tense as she listened intently to the recording play out and the information on the screen.

As this played out and the dispatcher initiated contact with the police and paramedics, Megan watched the call on the screen as the dispatcher traced the location for emergency services. The signal mysteriously vanished two minutes after emergency services pinpointed the call's location.

Jack recognized the technique but maintained a poker face. It was the application they frequently employed, and he suspected a report from Gabriel was waiting for him at the Jackal.

The dispatcher's voice acknowledges the last location again and that the signal has vanished. The file continues, and the team listens as the radio files come to life, allowing them to hear the events

reported by police and medical personnel as they enter
and do an initial search of the warehouse. Then, the
files go silent.

Megan looked at Aldo, "The call was placed
before 8 p.m. Did you find a phone?"

Jack knew they wouldn't if they weren't quick
enough. The phone was burned to molten slag.

"No, the team has been informed that it's still
missing, and it's a priority to find it and the person
who made the call," Aldo responded.

"So someone called 911, maybe smashed the
phone and tossed it." Megan looked at the forensic
team, which Oz delegated to as they worked. "Expand
the perimeter for the phone," Megan ordered them.
They all nodded and returned to work, with several
agents heading outside to expand the search.

"Think we have a witness?" Aldo inquired.

"Maybe. Did the dispatcher find anything on the number?" Megan turned to Kari, who was reviewing the dispatcher reports on the laptop.

Kari tapped the computer, checking the notes. "Burner number, nothing else on file—cheap sim, probably preloaded and bought in bulk. Anything helpful is likely long gone."

The frustration was visibly etched on Megan's face.

"Hold it right there!" an agent shouted from outside.

Megan and Kari bolted outside, following the agent. Jack trailed behind and stopped as he identified the person they were chasing. A subtle smirk graced Jack's lips. The recognition was evident from the individual's clothing. The fleeing figure was the same

person who had been spying on them.

Chapter 13

Wearing a black hooded sweater, black jeans, and white and red sneakers, the hooded figure sprinted away from the three ICIS agents at top speed. Megan was in hot pursuit, the hooded figure having just vaulted over the fence, the agents following closely. Kari was quick on their heels, taking a direct approach. Megan, however, split off to anticipate the suspects' possible route, attempting a shortcut to box them in. Scaling a small storage shed, she regained sight of the elusive stranger. Seizing the moment, she dashed up an alley. The agent closed in, aiming for a tackle, but the hooded person skillfully dodged. Glancing back and spotting Kari, the mysterious figure swiftly ducked into a small alcove. Ensuring no one was watching, the figure turned into a dark fog and ascended the wall, vanishing from sight. Kari and

Megan converged on the same spot from opposite sides, scanning the surroundings.

"Fuck," Megan said, catching her breath.

The dark fog traversed the rooftops, seamlessly flowing across three more buildings before retaking a human shape. With a sinister smile, the enigmatic figure gracefully descended to the ground, only to be confronted by Jack as they attempted to exit the alley.

"That's not very nice. You shouldn't spy on people," Jack remarked.

The hooded figure unveiled his face, revealing a cocky young man with dishevelled hair and intense dark eyes. As Jack scrutinized the figure and the extraordinary abilities he wielded, it became apparent that he was a supernatural being, commonly referred to as an SB in non-human circles. These entities were straight from legends and folklore, existing in an almost underworldly lifestyle hidden from ordinary humans. "You're not human," the man acknowledged Jack, recognizing the unnatural aura about him. However, Jack was different. While supernatural beings could quickly identify each other, the hooded man couldn't discern who or what Jack was.

Jack nonchalantly shrugged. "Who knows?"

The man wiped his face with his sleeve. Jack noticed a familiar mark on the man's hand that he had seen recently, the bastardized symbol of an ancient sun from the pamphlet. "Do you believe?"

"Believe? Probably not. Let me guess, the light? You let him in?" Jack speculated.

The man lifted his head, a smile playing on his lips. "Yes, and it was glorious. Brother, you should open your eyes."

"Why the two men? Why did they have to die?" Jack inquired.

He cackled, "A message to the false one that his time has finished."

"The false one. You mean the club owner?"

"Yes!"

"Hmm," Jack pondered.

"Brother, let him in, join in his light!"

Jack sighed, "If what you say is true, why would someone of light ask you to do something as dark as murdering two men, potentially damning you?"

"He didn't ask this of us. He said the heathens would need to be disposed of. We could eliminate one, and he would cleanse us of the sins committed. So we volunteered to do it." He laughed wickedly, smiling again.

"So, why follow the police?"

"To create a distraction if they got close," he boasted, then scowled, "the stupid human got suspicious and chased me."

"Yes, the stupid human..." Jack shook his head. "Or perhaps you're the one lacking intelligence?"

"Huh?" He appeared baffled.

"An SB like you, and you still know very little." Jack peered deep into the man's eyes. "You accuse someone of being evil, yet you don't even know what he looks like." Jack's eyes flickered with excitement as the realization struck the man.

"You can't be..."

"You recognized me as an SB but not for what I truly am. And you? You're a deathstalker."

"Claws that can kill, like infinitely sharp metal," he smirks. "I guess that makes you helpless."

"You fool." Jack's eyes flashed with rage. The deathstalker's smile faded. "This is a vessel for my power. Now, I wish I could unsheathe the blade hidden in my cane. Cut you up and make you truly regret the decisions you've made in the last few days..." At that moment, the world began to bend around the two men like an eclipse, a mesmerizing dance of light entwined with darkness. Jack stared deep into the man's eyes, allowing the deathstalker to see his features fully. His face appeared crazed, his smile morphing wider than humanly possible, reminiscent of the Cheshire cat from Alice in Wonderland, twisted and hungry for blood. The deathstalker was sweating bullets, immobilized. "...however, I can't return covered in blood, so you'll witness what I can do without a second thought."

Shadow tendrils extended from behind Jack toward the deathstalker in his human form, coiling grotesquely around him as Jack's eyes glowed eerily, his head slowly tilting to the side and his broad smile jagged and twisted. The deathstalker attempted to scream as the shadows squeezed tight and his physical essence burned away, but only silence ensued as the shadows devoured him entirely. The shadow tendrils receded into the ground, where Jack's shadow stood, and faded as Jack turned and walked away quietly. The shadow of Jack on the ground slowly licked its lips as

it disappeared back to normality.

Chapter 14

Jack slipped inside the dimly lit sanctuary of his club, his calm facade concealing a storm of emotions raging within him. Emerging from the chaos of the crime scene, he crafted a deceptive tale for Megan, spinning a web of deceit about joining the pursuit and taking another route to outsmart their elusive suspect. Megan insisted on detailed descriptions from all agents for an accurate APB on the suspect. They would never find him, not even a trace. Jack knew their quarry would forever remain uncaptured, a ghostly spectre dancing on the edges of their investigation. Leaving a generic description, Jack requested to return to his club and swiftly disentangled himself from the scene, his mind already consumed by the weighty matters awaiting his attention.

Navigating the winding corridors of his

establishment, Jack's footsteps echoed against the

freshly polished floors, each step a testament to the

clandestine dealings unfolding in the shadows.

Arriving at his secluded office in the club's depths, he

deftly manipulated a seemingly innocuous framed

painting, unveiling the concealed depths of a

meticulously hidden safe. With practiced precision, he

opened the safe. He placed his hand on the floor inside

it, activating the hidden scanner and casting an

ethereal glow across the room as the scanner approved

his access. A secret compartment emerged from its

slumber. Retrieving a note left by his confidant nestled

within the recesses of the safe's hidden compartment,

Jack unfolded it and perused its contents. "It's fine,

and I did find a lead in the investigation," he remarked

calmly, sensing the familiar presence of someone approaching the doorway.

As Jack turned, the stalwart figure of Gabriel, his unwavering sentinel, materialized in the doorway, a beacon of steadfast loyalty amidst the shadows and nightmares they regularly encountered. "Are you unharmed?" Gabriel's voice cut through the silence, laced with genuine concern and unwavering devotion.

Offering a reassuring nod, Jack's gaze locked with Gabriel's as he retrieved the cryptic cult pamphlet from his pocket. "Yes, Gabriel. All is well," he affirmed, a faint glimmer of resolve flickering in his eyes as he passed the pamphlet into Gabriel's waiting hands.

Gabriel was accustomed to the shadows, finding solace in their embrace. As a sentinel, he had pledged his life to safeguarding humans. When

Gabriel encountered Jack and uncovered his secrets, he made a solemn vow to protect him above all else. Despite facing rejection from his family for this decision, Gabriel remained steadfast, knowing it was the right path. He learned Jack held a pivotal role in the world's destiny, his existence serving as a linchpin upon which fate teetered precariously. Yet, his true identity remained shrouded in secrecy to everyone, even Gabriel.

The unexpected encounter between Megan and Jack signalled a shift in the tides. The world would soon be in imminent chaos, and these two would have destiny-altering choices they would eventually need to make. Gabriel possessed fragments of knowledge regarding the impending events, but Jack operated strictly on a need-to-know basis, and for now, it was not yet time for Gabriel to be privy to all the details.

Furthermore, Jack felt no obligation to reveal Megan's true destiny to her.

As Gabriel cast a disdainful glance at the cult-like membership pamphlet and its hidden meaning, Jack divulged more details. "Deathstalkers were responsible for their deaths. It was a direct message to me."

"What transpired exactly?" Gabriel inquired.

"I dispatched one of them. It trailed the police to disrupt any progress they made. If we are to comprehend the creature's dying words, it suggests the involvement of at least two more of these creatures."

"Did Ms. Briar witness your actions?"

"No, I used my shadow to prevent any traces of blood," Jack explained.

"I see. I've taken the liberty to establish the trust fund for the second victim," Gabriel informed him.

"Ensure it's substantial. The driver left children behind, and I want to ensure they are properly educated if they desire."

"Shall I adhere to the usual terms?" Gabriel inquired.

Jack settled into his seat behind the desk. "Yes, set up funds for a full scholarship or offer a lesser amount as an inheritance, one for each child, depending on their preference."

Gabriel scrutinized the pamphlet once more. "Should we be concerned about this?"

"I stumbled upon it at Mr. Stithulf's residence. He was human. It could pose a problem if humans are gaining access to forbidden knowledge. Interestingly, the deathstalker was also affiliated with the group. He possessed that mark on his hand," Jack explained.

"Do you suspect the victim had joined their ranks?" Gabriel inquired.

"I can't say for certain. But given the messages directed at me, it's imperative to meticulously review all incoming shipments, especially those containing alcohol," Jack replied.

"Speaking of which," Gabriel handed Jack a sleek, high-tech bracelet. "These have arrived, and we've thoroughly tested each one."

Jack inspected the bracelet. "Any issues during testing?"

Gabriel reported, "We confirmed their functionality at 100%, with all parameters falling within normal ranges."

A faint smile graced Jack's lips. "Excellent. These will prove invaluable for implementing my business strategy."

"Could you refresh my memory on the plan?" Gabriel requested.

Jack raised the bracelet. "Upon entry, patrons will be required to don this elegant accessory. They'll then enjoy complimentary drinks of their choice. Once the light changes colour, it will indicate a blood alcohol level outside the parameters. At this point, they'll be discreetly cut off from further alcohol consumption. However, they're encouraged to stay and indulge in other offerings like our cuisine, non-alcoholic beverages, live entertainment, and more."

"All at no charge?" Gabriel sought clarification.

"Indeed, Gabriel. I've been around long enough to know that cost is irrelevant, and these bracelets have a low tolerance threshold. If anyone causes trouble, they'll swiftly learn that long-term bans aren't desirable and this is the place to be. My aim is to contribute positively to our community. This city could benefit from a reminder of compassion and generosity," Jack affirmed.

Gabriel nodded, accepting the bracelet from Jack. "Is there anything else you require, sir?"

Jack flipped through a checklist of preparations needed for the club's opening. "Yes, secure a competent cook. That's one of the final pieces we need. And outside the club, make it a priority to track down those deathstalkers. We'll need to deal with them."

"Understood, sir," Gabriel acknowledged.

"And Gabriel."

"Yes, Sir?" Gabriel asked.

"Next time we encounter them, be ready, my dear sentinel, for you see, there will be blood." Jack cast a final glance at the symbol on the pamphlet Gabriel held. This situation was more profound than he had anticipated. The barrier between worlds seemed thinner than ever, and he had already made contact with others like him. Time was of the essence. They were drawing closer.

Chapter 15

Megan turned the key in the lock, stepping into the warm embrace of her home. The enticing scent of dinner greeted her, swirling through the air like a comforting melody.

"Hello, my love," Devlin's voice called from the kitchen. His figure appeared in the doorway adorned with a playful 'Kiss the Cook' apron. "How was your day?"

"Long," Megan sighed, sinking into the plush cushions of the couch. She reached for the chilled wine waiting in the bucket, a thoughtful gesture from Devlin. "That guy I was worried about? He's assisting us now."

Devlin emerged from the kitchen, eyebrows raised in surprise. "Seriously? Can they just do that?"

"They sure can, apparently," Megan replied with a defeated shrug, sipping the rich, velvety wine. Her gaze drifted to the table, where dinner awaited, a sight that brought a smile to her lips. "Aww, baby, you made dinner," she cooed, rising to give him a grateful hug.

"You worked your butt off today. Don't forget to recharge before diving back in," Devlin said, raising his beer in a toast as the glass clinked. She kissed Devlin's cheek lovingly before they settled down to eat.

After dinner, Devlin insisted on tackling the dishes and showering Megan affectionately with his lips before heading off to work.

As Megan prepared for bed, she slipped under the covers, the soft fabric enveloping her like a gentle caress. She switched on the sound machine, its soothing tones mimicking the gentle patter of raindrops.

Slowly drifting into slumber, Megan found herself in a dreamy downpour, relishing the cool touch of rain on her skin. But amidst the rain, a sense of unease crept over her. In the distance stood two figures, one hunched over and trailing scarlet rivulets as he knelt.

Approaching cautiously, Megan's heart quickened as she recognized Jack, a wicked sinister grin dancing on his lips as he brandished a blade. It was thrust through the slumped figure before him. She slowly crept closer, trying to look at Jack's victim. Horror gripped her as she realized his target: Devlin, impaled through the heart by Jack's twisted weapon.

Gasping for air, Megan felt suffocated, a whirlwind of voices and whispers swirling around her in a dizzying storm. Clutching her throat, she struggled to breathe, darkness encroaching on all sides.

Amidst the chaos, a single voice pierced through with startling clarity. "It's your destiny to protect him!" The words echoed thunderously, jolting Megan awake in a clammy sweat, her heart racing with fear.

Chapter 16

The following morning, Megan entered the war room, still haunted by the remnants of the disturbing nightmare. She sought solace and headed for the coffee machine, craving a caffeine boost to dispel her unease. As the rich aroma of brewing coffee filled the air, she focused on the task ahead, uploading the case file in anticipation of the upcoming meeting and eager to delve into the latest notes.

Aldo had completed the autopsy on the second victim, Mr. Abner Boone, yielding nothing but frustration once again. Despite meticulous examination, no traces or forensic evidence had emerged to unravel the mystery. Adding to the complexity was the puzzling inclusion of a mysterious 911 call and the missing phone that made it, further deepening the enigma.

As Megan reviewed the case notes on the computers, Jack appeared in the doorway. His presence instantly commanded attention; he casually hung his hat and jacket and offered Megan a courteous nod of acknowledgment.

"Hello, Agent Briar," he greeted.

"Jack, now isn't the best time. Have you reconsidered offering your assistance on this case?" Megan's tone conveyed her growing exasperation.

"No, my aid remains at your disposal until this case is resolved and I regain full permission to reopen my club," Jack asserted firmly.

"Approved. Go ahead and reopen!" Megan's frustration was palpable.

With a shake of his head, Jack persisted, "Why are you so adamant against my involvement? Do you still suspect I am responsible somehow?"

"Not responsible, but involved," Megan clarified.

Jack regarded her with a bemused expression. "Would you like me to return to the interrogation room?" he quipped.

Megan sighed wearily. "It's unlikely to serve our case unless you have new information to share."

Taking a seat at the table, Jack maintained his composure. "You were briefed on my discoveries yesterday. We uncovered the letter, and I provided a description of the runner. Unless you're interested in my dinner and breakfast schedules, there's been no significant development."

Megan furrowed her brow, still unable to decipher the enigmatic figure before her. Jack's attire, a fusion of modern and vintage styles, hinted at his complex persona, considerable wealth, and impeccable record. It was as if he harboured a more profound, darker secret lurking beneath the surface.

Just as the tension began to mount, Kari and Oz burst into the room, their excitement palpable.

"We've got something. The cameras caught a glimpse of the runner, enough for a match. It's being uploaded to our case now," Kari announced, passing a file to Megan.

Perusing the contents, Megan's eyes lit up with newfound determination. "Serafim Zhukov, aged 28, with ties to Russian crime but went off the grid 15 months ago. Let's track down his last known whereabouts and bring him in."

Finally, a breakthrough. Megan sighed in relief, but little did she know this lead would never fully pan out. Serafim was devoured by darkness and was gone for good.

Chapter 17

Jack stood beside Oz, peering through the one-way glass as Megan and Kari ushered in a procession of Serafim Zhukov's known associates, one after another, attempting to ascertain his location. The room buzzed with tension, filled with the palpable scent of anxiety mingling with the faint aroma of coffee drifting from the nearby break room. Mostly of Russian descent, the men and women clashed with the sterile atmosphere of the interrogation room. Some wore faces etched with defiance and suspicion, furious for being brought in. A few spat venom at the agents for their problems, knowing Serafim and welcoming him into their inner circles. Several attempted to sway Megan and Kari with bribery offers for his location, their voices laced with desperation and frustration, but to no avail.

Despite their efforts, interrogating those who came in yielded no answers.

Jack observed for two reasons. Firstly, to follow the case's information trail, knowing Megan might exclude him from the loop and that their search was focused on Serafim's whereabouts. Secondly, he sought elements beyond their investigation's scope, focusing on potential supernatural connections, especially those tied to this mysterious group. Noting few SBs among the suspects, with most being mortals caught in Serafim's network, none displayed signs of being a deathstalker or bore the mark signifying allegiance to this cult of light. Yet, during his personal interrogation with Serafim, a chill swept through Jack, accompanied by an acrid taste of apprehension lingering in the air. Serafim's gaze held a shadow, hinting at darker ties that piqued Jack's curiosity. It suggested a deeper connection between Jack and the light referenced in the pamphlet found in Mortimer Stithulf's residence. Jack had not witnessed such intensity in anyone else brought in.

Aware of the delicate balance between secrecy and revelation, Jack kept his suspicions close, careful not to expose the supernatural underbelly of their world to unsuspecting humans. SBs were primarily involved in this case, and Jack understood the potential repercussions of such knowledge getting out—paranoia, chaos, and the erosion of the human psyche. Yet, he also recognized the autonomy of SBs, some striving to maintain peace by keeping the truth concealed and living their lives. Others risked this balance by doing as they pleased in the shadows, causing new stories and lore about monsters, endangering both worlds.

As Kari escorted in the next suspect, Jack's keen eyes caught sight of a peculiar tattoo adorning the man's hand: three bastardized ancient suns resembling the one from the pamphlet. This man was a deathstalker, too.

Megan flipped through a file as Kari sat beside her. "Your name is Kostya Alexeev, correct?"

"Yes." Kostya sat firmly, avoiding direct eye contact and looking ahead between the agents.

"And you know Serafim Zhukov, correct?" Megan tapped the desk, peering into the man's eyes.

"He is an acquaintance of mine, yes." Kostya maintained a firm posture.

"Would you happen to know where he is?"

"I have not seen him in years."

"Well, we think you may have seen him sooner than that." Tension in the room crackled as Megan grilled the man.

"We think you may be hiding him," Kari said, a slight smirk on her lips, attempting to throw him off balance.

"I have not seen him in many years. I am sorry."

"You have ties with the Russian crime families, don't you?" Megan leaned on the table, spreading photos from the file for Kostya to see. Jack could make out the photos of him from through the glass. Some with high-ranking Russian mob members, pictures of Kostya with Serafim and even photos of Kostya heading into locations likely used as secret meeting spots.

"I have worked hard to clean my foul life. Those ties are behind me now."

Kari laughed at him, "Nobody can just leave a life like that."

"Are you sure that's the story you want to tell us? That you are reformed?" Megan looked at him suspiciously.

Kostya finally looked Megan in the eyes. "I worked hard for the status I have. It meant truly turning my life around, and I finally have happiness. I have a true family and good aspirations for the future. It was not easy, but I accomplished it. You are correct that I know Serafim. I had hoped he would have had the drive to be free. But he chose instead to run. If I see him again, I will contact your department."

Megan was irritated. She slipped her card onto the table, "For your sake, I hope that being clean is not a lie. I will lock you up if you slip."

"Yes, ma'am." Kostya picked up the card as an agent approached to escort him out.

Jack could see Kostya was angry as he exited the room. Jack excused himself as Oz finished making notes for the case.

Seeing Kostya at the elevator, Jack approached him quietly, stopping directly behind him. "I just wanted you to know he suffered. And the others will, too."

Kostya's eyes flared with anger, his fist tightening as Jack spoke, but he kept looking towards the elevator as the door opened. Jack had just laid the groundwork to find the killers for himself.

Chapter 18

Returning to the Jackal, Jack entered his office and gathered his files. The crisp sound of paper shuffling echoed in the quiet space. Checking his notes meticulously, he stepped into the dimly lit dining area of the club, greeted by the soft glow of ambient lighting that enveloped the room.

A young man anxiously waited in the dining area for his interview. His light brown hair, tousled and unkempt, caught the soft glow of the ambient lighting, framing his youthful features. There was a palpable sense of tension in his demeanour, a subtle awkwardness that emanated from his stiff posture and fidgeting fingers. Glancing around with uncertain eyes, he wore a tentative smile, revealing the inner apprehension that churned within him. Despite his efforts to appear composed, an undeniable air of unease clung to him, casting a shadow over the subdued atmosphere of the room.

"Hello, Sir! Thank you for this opportunity. I'm so honoured to have you try my food," said the young man eagerly as Jack approached, his voice brimming with enthusiasm as he vibrated with excitement.

Jack stopped in his tracks, his senses alert as he scrutinized the young man before him. "You're...dead," he remarked bluntly.

The man raised a finger. "We prefer undead, but yes, Sir. You have a good eye, for I am a ghoul," he confirmed, his tone carrying an undertone of pride as he awkwardly adjusted his collar.

Jack couldn't help but roll his eyes. "You're still dead. How can you cook when you can't taste properly?" he questioned skeptically, his voice laced with incredulity.

The ghoul, undeterred, offered his explanation. "You're right. My tastebuds are not functional. But I can assure you that I have trained hard to fulfill my passion for becoming a master chef," he replied earnestly, his hands nervously fidgeting with the hem of his apron.

Jack sighed in resignation. "I can appreciate your passion," he started, rubbing his right temple with his fingers, "but I swear to bloody hell, if this dish ends up killing me or any of my guests, I'll stab you in the face." His eyes narrowed, a sharp intensity cutting through the tense atmosphere.

The ghoul gulped nervously, his skin becoming pale, betraying a hint of apprehension. "Sir, I believe in my work. If you would please try the dishes," he implored, his eagerness palpable despite his nerves.

The young man extended a hand and presented several domed plates on the table. As Jack looked at the display, the young man lifted the domes, revealing inviting dishes that looked and smelled good.

Jack relented, picked up a fork, and tasted the food. The explosion of flavours on his palate surprised him. He cocked his eyebrow. *How the hell does a ghoul with no taste buds make a meal like that?* "Your name?" he inquired, genuine curiosity creeping into his voice.

"My name? It's...uh...Michael."

"Michael, what?"

"Um..." he looked at Jack nervously, "please don't laugh."

Jack looked at him blankly, lifting a glass of water to cleanse his palate.

The ghoul hesitated momentarily before responding, "My name is Michael David Dedley." His words were measured and deliberate.

Jack's reaction was immediate, his sudden shock causing him to spit out his water involuntarily. The table and spread were now drenched, and Jack choked, trying to get air. When he catches his breath, he looks at Michael. "Your last name is Deadly?" he exclaimed incredulously, his disbelief evident in his tone.

The ghoul responded nervously, "Yes, Dedley. It's spelled D-E-D-L-E-Y."

Jack shook his head in disbelief. "You're joking, right?" he questioned, still trying to believe the peculiar coincidence.

"No." Michael pointed at the plates slowly, "so, about the food?"

"Hang on. How did you get the name Dedley?"

"Oh... well, it was an unusual twist of fate. I was adopted by the Dedleys, a small family."

Jack couldn't help but chuckle internally at the absurdity of the situation. "They don't have a clue, do they?" he inquired, amusement evident in his voice.

The ghoul shook his head earnestly. "No, My parents have no idea I'm a ghoul," he confessed, a hint of guilt in his voice as he lowered his head.

Jack composed himself but desperately tried not to laugh directly in the young man's face.

"Sir, what are your thoughts on the food?" Michael motioned to the dishes again.

Despite the mess of water on the dishes and table, Jack raised his fork and tasted another dish, his senses alive with the intricate blend of flavours dancing on his tongue. "How did you do it?" he inquired, genuine curiosity colouring his voice.

The ghoul revealed his secret with a hint of pride. "Well, Ghouls can be born with unique skills."

"Must be very unique."

"Yes, it is. If we touch a body part, we can use them like our own. For example, I can use an eye to see through it or an ear to hear through it." he explained matter-of-factly.

"And a tongue you can taste through it?" Jack looks at him, a little disturbed.

"Exactly."

"So you have a rotting tongue on your person, for the sake of taste-testing my food…" Jack looked at the plates, even more disgusted by the thought.

Michael, taken aback by the comment, reached into his bag, pulling out a small jar. Inside was a tongue and a clear liquid. "I'll have you know it's fresh. I preserved it. I also use it like a proper chef would; I use a tasting spoon or plate to use the tongue. That's then placed with the dirty dishes immediately to be washed." He swished the small tongue-filled jar before Jack as if it were a regular act, showing him the small pink appendage.

"I guess that isn't as disgusting as I thought. But people's tastes are different. The tongue is refined, I assume?"

"Its previous owner was a master chef, yes." He grinned, sharing his forethought in finding a talented appendage to use his culinary passion.

Jack rolled his eyes and sighed. "Don't fall apart, don't do anything disgusting, and don't get caught by the other staff. If you can do that, then you're hired."

"Really?!" Michael grinned excitedly. The ghoul thanked him, his gratitude palpable as he eagerly anticipated the opportunity ahead.

"Yes. What you are doing... well, it's disgusting, but I suppose it is admirable. Just follow the rules." Jack adjusted his vest and headed to a list left on the bar. He crossed head chef off the list, then lower down highlighted that he still needed a hostess and a head bartender. He added a note returning it to its place for Gabriel to see upon his return. Having accomplished that task for opening night, Jack returned to his office

to work on other matters that required his attention.

Chapter 19

Gabriel had received a text from Jack earlier that day, asking him to follow Kostya and providing a photo for identification. Jack had tasks to handle at the club before opening, so he relied on Gabriel's tracking skills for this specific task. As Gabriel arrived at the Woodstock ICIS branch, he spotted Kostya Alexeev leaving and hailing a cab.

Watching Kostya's departure, Gabriel noticed the faint scent of cigarettes mixed with the hum of city traffic. Despite his role being to defend and protect, Gabriel recognized Jack's competence on his own. It had taken time for Gabriel to accept his role as more of a glorified assistant, but he firmly believed this would change. Something had drawn him to align himself with Jack years ago, and he trusted that destiny would not disappoint.

The cab pulled away, and Gabriel discreetly followed in his rundown white Mazda, a vehicle he used explicitly to remain inconspicuous on the job. They drove towards the city's outskirts for some time, with Gabriel keeping his distance. The objective was clear: Jack had observed signs linking this man to the cult of the light during the interrogation. Moreover, he was also a deathstalker. They needed to find out the next step for the other side.

Deathstalkers were primarily known for assassination and typically left little evidence behind. However, when they were killing in their monstrous natural form, they did leave behind some traces of evidence. More than the complete lack of evidence left behind, teams were found at the crime scenes. This puzzled Jack and Gabriel initially. However, upon realizing that the cult had a human element, Jack understood that they were still somewhat concealing their actual forms from the general populace and were cleaning up the crime scenes after their attacks. This suggested they might be waiting for the right moment, and revealing themselves prematurely to humans could jeopardize their plan. With these factors in mind and their improved understanding of the supernatural angle of the ICIS case they were involved in, things now made more sense.

The cab eventually stopped in the warehouse district, and Kostya stepped out. Gabriel parked and exited the car at a safe distance from the building. As a sentinel, he had enhanced senses, which allowed him to be more alert to his surroundings. This made the times he assisted in Jack's work as a private investigator invaluable.

Choosing a stealthier approach, Gabriel used his abilities and quietly jumped high into the air, landing silently on the roof and slipping through an open window. Inside, he cautiously navigated onto a small catwalk and gingerly stepped deeper in, the faint scent of ozone tickling his nose as he crept further. Eventually, Gabriel spotted Kostya conversing with two other men and made his way close enough to gather evidence. Pulling out a small camera, he secretly captured images of all the men, ensuring faces were visible for identification purposes.

Gabriel observed as Kostya entered a room full of people in dark robes praying toward a large altar. In the dim light, Gabriel could make out some of their hands and noticed that the same symbol from the pamphlet was on most of them. Meanwhile, Kostya was welcomed by a small group of men near the entrance, shaking hands and hugging them as they talked and laughed.

At the center of the group behind the altar, high enough for all to see, was a small glowing rift that emitted cosmic energy into the room as everyone chanted around it. This was the source of the ozone that Gabriel had detected earlier, and it was slowly bleeding cosmic energy, expanding into the room. A man came into view in white robes adorned with strange red symbols matching the suns Gabriel kept seeing; other than it matching the one on the pamphlet and marking its members, Gabriel didn't know its meaning or origins.

The white-robed man walked to the center of the room and stood at the altar to address the group. With his arms raised, he spoke, "Oh holy light, grant us strength as we navigate to the better world we know is coming. We offer our will to you, seeking eternal freedom that you have graciously offered us."

"Praise the light," the group responded and repeated three times in unison.

The man continued, "Brothers and sisters, We must remain vigilant against the signs we were forewarned of. The dark ones return to the eternal battlefield, and we have seen these signs!"

"Death to the false ones, death to the dark one, praise the light," they chanted.

"We had a special mission, one we undertook: to send a message to the dark one that he is unwelcome here and must return to where he came from."

"Praise the light, death to the dark one, praise the light," they echoed.

"However, it is with a sad and heavy soul that I report today our brother has fallen! A nonbeliever associated with law enforcement claimed he suffered by his hand!" The white-robed man shouted.

Gasps filled the room as the man spoke, and the robed people stopped praying and raised their heads in concern.

"I know this is scary to you all. But our brother Serafim was devoted to our cause. He is at peace. He is one with the light now," the white-robed man reassured his congregation.

All the robed figures started bowing at this declaration and chanting again: "Praise the light." They repeated as they bowed and prayed to the altar.

"We have chosen volunteers to retaliate, while the rest must remain vigilant. Our guiding light wishes to speak to us and has a plan for us all."

"Death to the false ones, death to the dark one, praise the light," they chanted again three times before falling silent.

The white-robed man bowed, stepping away slowly and kneeling to face the rift. Slowly, blue energy drifted out from its core, and a voice emanated from the flares and ripples it created.

"Believe in me. Rewarded in light. Our world is coming. I will smite them all." The energy flowed strongly for a moment at the declaration, then slowly rescinded like a wave returning to sea. "Sorry, my children. Not yet time."

Gabriel discreetly recorded a video of the events transpiring below him. Silence from the rift started the chanting again; Gabriel decided to exit while everyone was distracted again. This evidence would suffice for now.

As Gabriel approached the open window, he overheard someone calling for Kostya below him. He stopped and listened quietly, crouching on the catwalk near his escape.

"Orders have been given, sir." A black-robed man approached him with a file in hand.

"Yes?"

"We eliminate this unit and erase our trail. All humans are to be killed without leaving a trace." The man handed Kostya the file, and he opened it, seeing the photos of team two and several other ICIS members who were closing in on identifying members of the cult.

A chilling smile spread across Kostya's face. "I'll take care of the bitch and the one who killed our brother."

Gabriel calmly slipped out and hurried to his car. Jack needed to be informed promptly that danger was coming.

Chapter 20

After a long day filled with interrogations and a positive identification, Megan finally settled into bed. However, they still hadn't located where their suspect was hiding. She just needed to find his location to bring him in.

As her mind raced over the clues, she closed her eyes and started to dream. The soothing sound of waves washed over her, transporting her to a serene beach. She felt the soft sand beneath her feet and let the gentle breeze tousle her hair. Stepping slowly across the beach, enjoying the moment, it wasn't long before the next step turned to something grotesque. The texture of the sand changed, becoming slimy and unpleasant with each step forward, further twisting the landscape. Looking out at the sea, she was horrified to see the waves turning red, leaving a strange film on the shore.

Ahead, she spotted a figure and hesitantly approached. The air became a sickeningly metallic sweet smell. Drawing nearer, she recognized the figure as Devlin. Silently, she reached out and touched his shoulder. He turned to face her, but what she saw chilled her to the bone: his face was contorted and deformed, with a large, jagged barb protruding from his mouth.

"What troubles you, my love?" His voice was warped and unsettling.

As this nightmarish version of Devlin drew closer, a blade suddenly pierced his heart from behind. Devlin looked down at the blade tip and slowly collapsed, vanishing into the mix of bloody sand. Standing there behind where Devlin once stood was

Jack, his features obscured by his hat and a twisted smile on his face as blood dripped from the sky around them like gruesome rain.

"Danger, child, danger, child," the words repeated and echoed in her ears as she tried to scream. The voices continued until a hand gripped her shoulder, forcing her to turn. The voices stopped, and the world around her became a regular beach again. She found herself facing Jack again. He looked normal, but his expression was now grave.

He looked her deep in the eyes. "You're in danger, child," he warned, his voice urgent.

Megan was startled awake, bolting upright in bed, drenched in sweat, as the new day dawned outside her window.

Chapter 21

Early in the morning, Jack received an urgent message from Gabriel: 'ICIS in danger.' Stepping outside, he promptly dialled the ICIS dispatcher.

"Hello, Jack Blakely here," he said. "I'm consulting with team two in the specials division. I was about to head in but heard the team was called to a scene. Can you provide the address and update me on the situation?" he asked as he walked towards his car.

"Just a moment, Sir," the dispatcher replied. "Yes, they were dispatched to a reported murder scene not long ago. No one has arrived yet. I'll send you the address."

"Thank you very much," Jack acknowledged, ending the call. He immediately dialled Gabriel.

"I've sent you the address," Jack said. "I fear the agents might be walking into an ambush. Although reported as another murder, no one was on-site; it was called in. That isn't procedure."

"Any sign of activity at the Jackal?" Gabriel inquired.

"None," Jack replied, glancing around the area. He took a last scan of his abilities before sitting in the driver's seat of his velvet blue BMW M8.

"Are you heading there?" Gabriel asked.

"Yes, but this needs to be handled delicately," Jack explained. "If deathstalkers are planning to erase everyone they've determined is expendable, then they will reveal themselves as non-human. Things could escalate quickly."

"Understood. I'll proceed with discretion," Gabriel assured him.

Jack started his car, peeling out, heading towards the given address. Being closer to the Jackal meant Megan and team two had a head start. If the deathstalkers revealed themselves, the revelation would complicate everything and be challenging to explain.

Chapter 22

Gabriel arrived first, his senses sharpened as he surveyed the area. The abandoned high-rise towered ominously, its silence pregnant with foreboding. With urgency in his step, he dashed inside, his keen eyes scanning the derelict interior for any signs of trouble. Though no murdered bodies were present to greet him, Gabriel knew time was scarce.

Emerging from the building, a voice shattered the silence. "He's not one of them," it declared. Gabriel pivoted to behold one man approaching him in the doorway.

"Get him anyway, no witnesses," another barked from a different direction. These figures were the same individuals Kostya had encountered when Gabriel first entered the warehouse. Gabriel's intuition whispered that they were likely two of the dreaded deathstalkers.

"Pathetic worms," Gabriel taunted as he darted back into the building, hoping to lure them inside. Gabriel felt goading them on might be a way to keep them from prying eyes. He sprinted through the decrepit corridors, catching glimpses of his pursuers trailing close behind their supernatural speed, just managing to keep up with his current one.

The building's decayed state heightened the urgency as Gabriel raced up a staircase, each step echoing in the desolate space. His enhanced abilities granted him extraordinary speed, but the enclosed environment favoured the deathstalkers' elusive shifting technique. It was a skill that rendered them formidable assassins, enabling them to transform into dark fog to evade detection or strike swiftly. In this form, they could reach Gabriel much faster, even at his top speed, but he needed to keep them following him.

Ascending, Gabriel adjusted his strategy, using the railing to scale the stairs more rapidly. Suddenly, a noise below caught his attention, and he instinctively jumped onto the staircase above him and leaned back just in time to avoid a surge of black fog. Within the fog gleamed a blade. As the fog travelled upwards past him, the blade cut into the staircase below and above him, causing pieces of the damaged stairwell to crumble around him. They were relentless.

His phone buzzed, and a call from Jack connected to his earpiece, breaking the tension. "I'm busy, boss," Gabriel replied, undeterred by the chaos around him.

"Make it to the roof," the command echoed in Gabriel's earpiece before the call ended. The fog swirled around him, the deathstalkers alternating between tangible and ethereal forms, slashing through the air like hungry strays for a fresh kill. Undeterred, Gabriel spotted a sign indicating roof access. He veered in the opposite direction with a burst of speed, his enhanced agility guiding him as he dodged the deathstalkers' frenzied attacks. Their blows missed their mark, causing them to crash into the unyielding walls instead.

A triumphant grin played on Gabriel's lips; he flipped them off as he sprinted towards the rooftop exit. With a forceful push, he burst through the door, greeted by the vast expanse of the empty roof and no sign of Jack. However, his relief was short-lived as one of the deathstalkers swiftly caught up to him.

"Nowhere left to go, shield," one of them taunted, a sinister smirk on his lips.

The ground rumbled as Gabriel looked down. He watched the rooftop beneath his feet crack and the other deathstalker emerge, slashing through the infrastructure. Gabriel dodged out of the way just in time as the second deathstalker climbed out of his hole and stalked toward Gabriel. "Except down, broken and bloody," he chimed in, their laughter echoing in the desolate air as they cornered their prey on the roof.

A sense of unease crept over Gabriel. Stepping slowly back towards the edge, he glanced over his shoulder at the abandoned street below. He spotted Kostya below, watching with approval, alongside two other men armed with firearms. Gabriel's instincts warned him of the looming threat. He was anticipating an imminent assault from all sides and the three men climbing the building from the outside with their shift.

The heavy roof door closed with a resounding thud behind the two deathstalkers, Jack's hand firmly on the door looking at them. He stepped forward, regarding them with a mixture of disappointment and disdain.

"I'm disappointed. Two-on-one from the greatest assassin breed on the other side? Pathetic," he remarked, his voice laced with scorn.

Gabriel, ever vigilant, maintained his defensive position. "Five, Sir. Three below as well," he informed.

Jack shook his head, a furrow forming on his brow. "No, two are human. That's why they have guns. And this is where I have a problem. How is it that two humans know something sacred? Are we looking to start a new witch hunt? Scare the humans into hunting the monsters again?"

One of the deathstalkers glanced back at Jack, his expression defiant. "Our light lets all in. We serve and honour all; we are the chosen few who will see the new world."

Jack let out a resigned sigh, his frustration evident. "That's bloody fantastic, humans knowing what's out there in the shadows, in the name of a freak with a messiah complex promising the manna from heaven."

The deathstalker, fueled by fervour, turned and charged toward Jack. "Don't talk about our light!"

Quickly, Jack retrieved a thick, sharp sword from his cane. Turning a release on the handle, the sword delinked slowly, looking like it was falling apart.

Time almost slowed as the deathstalker yipped with glee, moving in for his strike, unaware of Jack's trickery.

As the deathstalker closed in, Jack lifted his hand and unleashed his weapon's hidden form—inside his trick cane was a lethal sword that doubled as a barbed whip. The deathstalker saw Jack's movements and confidence; his actions were now filled with doubt, and he moved to avoid any incoming strikes. However, with lightning speed, the chained blade slashed in multiple directions, catching the deathstalker off guard. It was too late for the deathstalker to react. With a pained shriek, he fell forward, his body slashed entirely as body parts and organs spilled on the rooftop beside where Jack stood. The deathstalker's corpse now spread like a smear of paint on the canvas of its twisted painter.

Jack walked to the edge where Gabriel stood; turning his gaze downward, Jack locked eyes with Kostya, who observed the scene from the street with anger and dismay, knowing he had lost one of his men but not how it happened.

As the second deathstalker recoiled in horror, Gabriel swiftly repositioned himself to block the door and the hole, confining the creature to the roof.

"Don't kill me!" the deathstalker pleaded with Jack.

Jack swiftly tapped his whip on the ground, the movement reverting the whip back into its sword form, and approached the creature on the roof. "You've made a grave mistake. You thought you acted for salvation, but it only led to your destruction," Jack continued, closing in on the other deathstalker. "And not only that, you threatened someone you shouldn't have."

"We'll leave you alone!" the deathstalker countered desperately.

"I don't mean the threat to me nor my shield," Jack replied firmly, snarling at the creature through his clenched teeth.

"Who then?!" the deathstalker demanded.

In a sudden movement, Jack flash-stepped towards the deathstalker, seizing him by the neck and holding him up for Kostya to see from the street below. Kostya watched as darkness enveloped Jack, his Cheshire smile twisted. Jack leaned down, towering over Kostya, his eyes glowing as he looked out of the corner of his eye, addressing the frightened creature in his hands. The deathstalker started to slash his sharp blades and thrust his tail at Jack, but as Jack's eyes started to glow, so did his powers begin to manifest on his body, and the shadows slowly started to cover the exquisitely dressed psychopath. And despite the deathstalker's attempts to break free, Jack's shadowy tendrils effortlessly thwarted each attack.

"You're the dark one, the false prophet!" the deathstalker whimpered.

"No. You've been lied to. I'm just the current king of this world. Bid farewell to the man who knows more than he lets on," Jack declared, presenting the deathstalker to Kostya. As Jack smiled his twisted, sinister smile down at Kostya, the shadows around him grew and became a sizeable fanged mouth of darkness devouring the offering he held, leaving no trace.

Jack smiled slowly and turned to leave Kostya's eyesight. He stepped towards the torn remains of the other deathstalker, and the shadows grew to feast once more on the scattered remains of the deceased cohort, the body slowly dissolving into the darkness that surrounded it. As the shadows slowly vanished into the ground, the rooftop was devoid of body, blood included, and completely clean. It left nothing behind.

Kostya's expression shifted from anger to horror as ICIS black SUVs arrived on the scene. Upon seeing Kostya and his armed men, Megan swiftly exited her vehicle, her M&P 2.0 in hand aimed at the suspects, and issued commands. "ICIS, weapons down and hands up!" she ordered.

Oz, Kari, and several other ICIS agents followed suit, guns drawn, barking demands at the three remaining men.

Kostya snarled and commanded his men, "Kill them, you idiots!" but they remained paralyzed by fear and confusion, yielding to the armed ICIS agents' demand for surrender. Realizing his plan had crumbled, Kostya hastily retreated into the alley amid the chaos.

Meanwhile, Oz and Kari swiftly moved to apprehend the men who had dropped their weapons and raised their hands in surrender. Megan dashed to the alley but found no sign of Kostya. Grabbing her radio, she urgently transmitted, "Agent Megan Briar here. Initiate an APB for Kostya Alexeev. He's armed and dangerous."

Megan looked to where the men were facing when they had arrived. She noticed they were looking upwards. Glancing up at the building roof, Megan puzzled over what had caught their attention earlier.

What the hell were they looking at before?

Having stepped back from the ledge alongside Gabriel, Jack turned to him, acknowledging his efforts. "You did well here."

Gabriel's concern lingered on Kostya. "What about Kostya?"

Jack's response was succinct. "You have your tasks for opening night... As do I."

Chapter 23

Megan directed the forensic team to meticulously comb through the dilapidated building. They scrutinized every inch, their gloved hands delicately probing for clues amidst the hushed atmosphere. Despite their thoroughness, nothing stood out as out of the ordinary.

The arrested men remained stubbornly silent, their lips sealed tight against any divulgence. Megan observed their stoic demeanour, noting the absence of legal representation. Their IDs revealed identities that didn't match her expectations— they were not Russian, adding another layer of complexity to the situation. She had braced herself for the involvement of the Russian mob or an internal power struggle within factions, given their escalating influence in the case. Then there was Jack; Jack's link to the victims hinted at a more profound significance. However, the men they arrested had no connection to Jack or the transportation company Milk & Honey.

As she pored over the file notes, Megan felt like she was peering through a keyhole into a vast, intricate tapestry of secrets. It was as if she was too close to one side of a Rubik's cube and was missing the other parts of the puzzle because it was flat in her perspective.

Erika strode purposefully into the war room, her steps resounding with determination. Taking her place beside Megan, she settled into a chair with a controlled grace. "Any developments on Kostya or Serafim?"

Megan's response came in the form of a slow, thoughtful shake of her head. "Something doesn't sit right. This doesn't feel like a win. It's as if we're nearing the end of a chapter, but I don't feel like I will

see the rest of this story. There are vital pieces of the

puzzle missing, being kept from me."

"What's leading you to that conclusion?"

"It's hard to articulate. Just a gut feeling.

Serafim Zhukov remains elusive. We've uncovered no

allies or contacts willing to speak favourably of him.

My suspicion? He may have been silenced to keep him

off our radar."

"By whom?"

"It's conceivable that Kostya Alexeev is

involved. Despite his professed reform, he was armed

and awaiting our arrival when we approached the

crime scene that was called in. But there's an

unsettling aura surrounding the entire situation."

"How so?"

"It felt like stepping into an ambush that had already been sprung, even though we hadn't reached the scene yet."

"An ambush targeting you and your team?"

"Yes. We received a tip about another body, matching the descriptions of the previous two crime scenes."

"But there wasn't a body at the scene?"

"No, which deepened my suspicion that it was a trap."

Erika tapped her pen against the table, lost in contemplation. "Your instincts might be onto something. What about Alexeev? Do you believe your team is in danger? There is still an active APB out for his arrest."

"I don't think so. Something makes me think we won't. It feels like there's a larger game being played."

"Given the circumstances, we've issued a warrant for his arrest. He threatened federal agents and has new weapons charges; that's enough to make him a candidate for our most wanted list. If any agencies can bring him in, he will go away for a long time. While I don't know if I agree it's the last we have seen of him, it should compel him to keep a low profile."

"Yes, ma'am."

Erika rose from her seat, her gaze lingering on Megan as she approached the door. "Take the night off. Give me your report tomorrow. Maybe it's time you visit your consultant. We've greenlit his opening for tonight."

"But I—"

Erika raised a hand, cutting Megan off. "This case has too many loose ends. If you run yourself ragged, you'll burn out. Learn when to step back. You're my top agent. Now, go unwind. That's an order."

With that, Erika exited the war room, leaving Megan with her thoughts and a cascade of unanswered questions.

Chapter 24

The park enveloped Kostya in an eerie darkness, punctuated by the flickering of lights and the ceaseless hum of insects. With a duffel bag slung over his shoulder, he hurried across the damp grass, each step muffled by the moist dirt. The rustle of leaves seemed amplified in the stillness, sending a shiver down his spine.

Suddenly, he caught the faint creak of metal from the nearby playground, and his heart pounded in his chest, a primal rhythm echoing the tension in the air. His eyes darted around, searching the darkness for dangers. He breathed a small sigh of relief and continued on his path of escape.

As he stepped toward his salvation, a figure materialized from the darkness, emerging stealthily from behind a gnarled tree directly in his path.

"Such an unpleasant night," remarked Jack, his voice slicing through the silence like a blade.

"Get away from me..." Kostya's voice wavered, his grip tightening on the strap of his bag.

Jack interrupted his plea, "Call me 'the dark one' again, and I'll snap your neck. You're higher up in your little cult; surely you realize it's all bullshit," Jack's gaze pierced through the gloom at Kostya.

Kostya set his bag down with a soft thud on the dewy grass, squaring his shoulders, his resolve hardening. "I'm aware enough."

"Good. You seem to have the answers. I appreciate that," said Jack, his tone almost mocking.

"I won't talk," Kostya spat, defiance lacing his words.

Jack stepped forward, his form looming ominously in the dim light. "Oh, but you will talk. Let's delve into the essence of the rift you all fervently worship. I possess insights into its nature, but do you?"

"If you already have the answers, why interrogate me?" Kostya snapped, his patience wearing thin.

"Because I require specifics. Without precise details, it's all mere conjecture. So, about the rift—have you communed with the entity residing on the other side?" Jack inquired, his voice low and insistent.

"Yes, and it pledged salvation," Kostya replied, his voice barely above a whisper.

"It deceived you," Jack said casually, lighting a tiny cigarette. He glanced at Kostya, drawing shapes with the lit tip in the air. "Allow me to tell you a tale..."

"Once upon a time, a race of formidable beings existed known as the Etherials. They held dominion over creation and annihilation, embodying existence itself. One day, the Etherials got bored, so they decided to watch a planet that intrigued them and gamble. They would select a species to place their bets on and see which would become the top of the food chain first, an alpha species. Life went on like this until, eventually, the Etherials became intrigued by humans. As they start learning about their new playtoy species, the Etherials discover they can even possess a human, increasing their influence further on the events of their wagers. As a result, the stakes grew higher, leading to conflicts and contests to showcase superiority. Over time, rules were established to regulate the game, resulting in a colossal conflict beyond anything chronicled in religious texts.

As the battles escalated, the Etherials reached an accord. Rules were made, enforced, adapted, and restructured to ensure fairness. The result was a war on a scale you have never seen but could only read about in religious and holy texts. The Etherials then agreed: rather than perpetual warfare among myriad cultures and beliefs, they would select two representatives—a vessel for themselves and a guardian to handle powers they could not. Yin to a Yang. The victor would wield absolute power, dictating the fate of the Earth until the dawn of the next war."

The air grew heavy as Jack spun his tale as Kostya looked on, each word laden with implication, like a suffocating fog. Kostya's expression grew angry as he listened. Jack leaned against the tree, his voice carried through the air as he continued.

"Inside that rift was someone making backroom deals. You've unwittingly danced under my reign as king for a while now, and I don't appreciate cheaters. And this light, this promised salvation... Picture this: one emerges victorious, wielding the power to reshape our world. How many faiths thrive in the world?"

"Many," Kostya conceded, the words laden with resignation.

"A scholar of the world, I see. Your world may not be perfect, but it's yours. I mean, hell, you didn't even know about me. I allowed every creature of the Earth to roam freely; I leave you all alone. But in the throes of war for the crown, say fortunes shift, they may change that. The world could be reverted back to servitude. Now, reflect on your history. Throughout time, people have claimed noble intentions and birthed devastation upon anyone who thinks differently. Sometimes, even the faithful suffer. So, tell me, if you kneel to your master and meet the executioner's blade, will you still find your salvation?"

Kostya snorted disdainfully, his breath a sharp exhale in the tense air.

"Did I tell a joke?" Jack probed, his tone like a serpent's hiss.

"Just you. Your fabrications. See, I know the truth," Kostya retorted, his voice a defiant whisper.

"Do you think so? I've dispatched three of your flock. They don't seem saved. Their cries, their screams—they pissed me off. In the end, no saviour came to their aid."

"They lacked true faith," Kostya sneered, a cruel smirk twisting his lips. "But I've been blessed with the name and purpose of my deliverer. They have not."

"Very well, let's put your faith to the test. Summon your saviour. Let the celestial wings carry you to salvation or whatever the fuck their method is," Jack taunted, his words sharp as a dagger's edge.

"And with his name, the dark one will tremble. His name is Shade. And he will bring you to your knees," Kostya declared boldly, his voice resonating with unwavering confidence.

Jack's smile faltered, a shadow crossing his features. "Still playing games. Whoever you invoke, it is not Shade. You've been deceived," Jack countered, his voice tinged with bitterness.

"And why is that?" Kostya grinned wickedly, sensing he had struck a nerve.

"Because Shade was cast out for breaking the rules. So either it truly is Shade—a tyrant, a bastard who enslaves all, offering only chains and servitude as he forces his position into an eternal spot. Or it's another Etherial using his name to get to me. Also, they are turning you into a pawn, a toy in their machinations. Either way, salvation eludes you. I'm sorry, truly, for it proves you're but an expendable piece in their game," Jack explained, his words a bitter truth hanging heavy in the air.

Anger simmered beneath Kostya's skin as he locked eyes with Jack, his glare piercing through the darkness. "But it did frighten you. I saw it," he insisted, his voice edged with accusation.

Jack chuckled, a low, sinister sound that echoed through the night. "I am the king, remember? If the mere mention of Shade makes me tremble, why was I the one to end him?" His gaze bore into Kostya's, intense and unwavering.

Kostya's face contorted with rage. "I saw your fear, false prophet!" he spat, his accusation slicing through the air like a dagger.

Jack closed his eyes, a solemn expression crossing his face. "I'm sorry, Kostya, but you're mistaken. I warned you to stop with the names. I was trying to rein in my bloodlust. You see, my vessel is ancient; it hasn't aged a day since our pact in London over a century ago."

"London?" Kostya echoed, his mind reeling with the revelation.

"Yes, near Whitechapel in 1886. How's your history?" Jack advanced, each step deliberate, as Kostya involuntarily retreated, the puzzle pieces falling into place.

As realization dawned, Kostya's face twisted in horror.

Jack's gaze bore down on him, a sinister smile curling his lips. "That's right, old boy. I had a well-known name back then. I even share similarities with it now," Jack advanced with a chilling purpose while Kostya struggled against encroaching shadows, "I'm Jack... The Ripper!"

Darkness swirled around Jack, blades spiking towards a helpless Kostya, resonating with Jack's malicious laughter. The world around them bent in a twisted consortium of light and dark. Instead of consuming Kostya entirely as he had with the others,

Jack's shadow became a relentless onslaught—a punishment for every innocent life taken. Death by one thousand cuts. As Kostya teetered on the edge of oblivion, his eyes flickering with fading vitality, he was impaled upon a final spike of darkness, cruel barbs jetting outward as a final infliction to hold him still. Only then did Jack's shadows consume him whole, erasing Kostya's monstrous presence from existence without a trace. With grim determination, Jack melted into the night's embrace, leaving a chilling void of darkness behind.

Chapter 25

Megan and Devlin arrived at the club, greeted by a pulsating wave of energy that enveloped them like a tangible force. Gabriel, the towering bouncer, stood at the entrance, commanding respect as he gracefully parted the plush velvet rope to usher them inside.

"Mr. Blakely extends a personal invitation to you and your fellow ICIS agents," Gabriel announced, his voice carrying over the thumping bass of the music. With a guiding hand, he ushered them through the crowd toward the VIP entryway. "Your colleagues are waiting inside."

With a flourish, Gabriel presented Megan with a sleek VIP pass, its glossy surface reflecting the colourful lights dancing around them. "Enter, present this to the hostess, and get fitted," he directed, gesturing toward the VIP hostess booth.

Approaching the desk, Megan and Devlin were met by a poised hostess whose warm greeting added to the electric atmosphere. "Welcome to the Jackal," she said with a smile. "I see that Mr. Blakely has granted you VIP status. May I see your hands, please?"

Megan and Devlin extended their hands as the hostess retrieved two sleek mechanical bracelets. Their metallic surfaces glinted under the club's vibrant lights as she snugly secured them around their wrists.

"Seems rather elaborate for a nightclub, doesn't it? Ouch!" Devlin remarked, wincing as the bracelet tightened unexpectedly.

"The experience at the Jackal is unique," the hostess explained, handing them informational leaflets. "Guests must adhere to the guidelines outlined in these flyers. You're entitled to two alcoholic drinks or less, as regulated by your wristbands. Everything, including the live entertainment, is complimentary."

Megan and Devlin exchanged incredulous glances. "Complimentary?!"

"Yes, the bracelets monitor your blood alcohol levels and track them to ensure safe ranges," the hostess confirmed. "The Jackal aims to provide a distinctive late-night experience, allowing customers to live as equals and try new things while eliminating financial concerns and maintaining a safe social environment."

"How does he make a profit?" Devlin quipped.

"Mr. Blakely awaits you in the VIP section," the hostess redirected, gesturing toward the staircase on the right.

Megan and Devlin began ascending to the VIP area. It had been a while since Megan had first walked these stairs and found Jack lurking in the shadows. As they approached their friends in the VIP area, Jack greeted them.

"Thank you for joining us, Agent Briar," Jack greeted Megan.

"Jack, how do you manage to charge nothing?" Megan inquired.

"We've discussed this before, Ms. Briar. And who's your companion tonight?" Jack asked.

"This is my boyfriend, Devlin Alastor."

Jack reached out and shook Devlin's hand. "It's a pleasure. Please relax and enjoy. The band will be starting soon."

As Jack departed the VIP area and headed down the stairs into the club's heart, Megan felt a shiver, sensing his intense gaze fixed on Devlin. Almost a penetrating stare through him. A voice snapped her attention out of her thoughts. Aldo and Kari's conversation about the club and atmosphere brought her back to reality.

"So, Megs, what's your take?" Aldo asked.

"It's certainly unique," Megan replied, her gaze drifting to Jack on the floor below them. She watched him shake hands and welcome guests.

Her suspicions lingered. Jack still bothered her. His allure intrigued her, yet her instincts simultaneously screamed to escape him. She was

fighting an internal battle to define him—was he a

benevolent patron or a crime lord?

Chapter 26

Jack sauntered confidently into the backstage area, where the musical band eagerly awaited him. Their faces alighted with anticipation as he approached.

"Hello there, everyone. How's everyone feeling?" Jack greeted warmly, his presence sparking excitement among the group.

"Ready to rock!" the drummer exclaimed enthusiastically. His enthusiasm was mirrored by the rest of the band as they cheered for Jack for being a gracious host.

"As you all know, I'm deeply impressed by your talent and artistry. I've long admired your work. I was wondering if I could join you for a song during your set if you're open to it. Hospitality has always been a cornerstone of my business philosophy, fostering

connections and creating memorable experiences for

all our guests," Jack said. His appreciation for the

band's skill was evident in his words.

The band looked at each other and nodded in

agreement. "If the crowd boos you off stage, does it

look bad on us?" The vocalist laughed jokingly.

Jack grinned and looked him in the eye.

Naming a track from the set list, he looked at the

guitarist, "Would you play the chorus?"

The guitarist picked up his guitar, strumming

out the chorus as Jack delivered a flawless rendition,

seamlessly blending his voice with the music. The

band clapped approvingly.

"Looks like I might have to eat my words if you keep this up!" the vocalist joked, joining in the applause from the rest of the band.

Jack reassured him with a pat on the shoulder. "No need to apologize. I understand the skepticism. After all, you're the artist. I am merely painting a single stroke on the canvas," he bowed respectfully.

"We'll catch you out there, Jack!" The band cheered eagerly, their excitement palpable as they prepared for their performance.

Exiting the dressing room, Jack strode purposefully toward his office to change into a different outfit. Gabriel entered, silently closing the door behind them.

"Sir?" Gabriel asked.

"I handled the situation. I've gleaned some insights, at least for now," Jack responded, his tone reflective as he shared his thoughts.

"Was it an Etherial?" Gabriel inquired, his concern evident in his voice.

"It seems someone is claiming to be Shade," Jack explained, his expression grave as he revealed his findings.

"And if it truly is Shade?" Gabriel pressed further, his apprehension growing.

"Then we'll handle him accordingly. He tried to upset the balance and sever the strength of the bloodlines. It would have weakened everyone, allowing him to retain his power eternally. I have never seen anyone escape banishment, but I suppose there is a first time for everything," Jack said, looking at Gabriel as he adjusted his vest. "If it is Shade, he won't be allowed to strategize unchecked. The battle for the crown seems to be beginning as destiny planned," Jack declared firmly, his resolve unwavering in the face of uncertainty.

Gabriel shifted uneasily as music and cheers filled the air, signalling the band's appearance on stage. Jack noticed Gabriel's nervous movements.

"Sir, if the conflict is beginning, perhaps we should..." Gabriel started, his concern evident.

"Relax. Yes, this is going to be a clash of titanic forces. The likes of which will shake the foundations of the world. But you can survive it; I am not worried," Jack reassured him, placing a reassuring hand on his shoulder before walking towards the door to leave.

"No, I was referring to your guardian," Gabriel began, but Jack interrupted, addressing his concerns.

"Yes, Gabriel, I'm aware. If I can avoid dragging my guardian into this battle of life and death, then I will." Jack turned and looked at Gabriel again. "Megan Briar will be given a choice regarding her involvement. If Megan uncovers her destiny, I will no longer keep it from her. If she doesn't, she'll remain shielded and unaware of the dangerous shadows lurking around her. But should Megan learn that she's destined to be the next guardian of the current king, she'll be entrusted with everything, and she'll have to make her decision," Jack affirmed, his commitment to respecting Megan's free will unwavering.

Gabriel moved forward in protest. "Sir, why? Guardians and keeping the balance are needed in order to maintain your chance of winning!"

Jack looked down with a strong sigh. "Because I have spent my time ruling, undoing the wrongs my family has done. Shade trying to enslave the world was wrong. This time around, I chose free will for the people. I spent my time experiencing life. She also deserves that right for as long as she can before it gets taken away from her."

With a solemn nod to Gabriel, Jack left the room and approached the stage, where the musical talent awaited. Stepping onto the stage, he greeted the audience and welcomed them to the club's grand reopening event. With a smooth transition, he joined the band, his rich voice blending effortlessly with the music.

Jack had always cherished music and art throughout his existence, watching humanity's ebb and flow through life and death. He spent a million lifetimes doing a million things and watched, letting

humanity run its natural course, only ever offering a

guiding hand. Jack had intervened to halt senseless

conflicts and prevent needless suffering. Yet, above all,

he championed the principle of free will, determined

to grant humanity the freedom to live and thrive.

Because in the past, Jack had seen those things taken

away: men, women, and children caged and chained

as prisoners like animals, living only to die. The least

he could do was let them enjoy the peace while it

lasted.

Jack's smile radiated warmth as the song's final

notes faded away. He graciously thanked the band and

waved to the audience. Stepping down from the stage,

he briefly glanced at Megan and the other agents in

the VIP area. However, a nagging concern lingered in

his mind. He sadly needed to maintain a vigilant

watch and stay out of it. Freedom to live. Respecting

the sanctity of Megan's choice, Jack had to relinquish

control and let her decide what the future would hold.

She had to make the choice herself.

Chapter 27

Megan returned home, tenderly kissing Devlin goodnight before bidding him farewell and preparing for bed. As she settled under the covers, she activated her sound machine. The soothing thunderstorm rumble enveloped the room, its low growl mingling with the soft patter of raindrops.

Drifting into sleep, Megan immersed herself in a vivid dream of a raging thunderstorm surrounding her. She marvelled at the power and awesomeness but knew she felt a strange sense of tranquillity. The cool breeze and the smell of damp soil calmed her nerves. Suddenly, amidst the swirling winds and crashing thunder, she spotted Jack standing before her.

"Go away!" she cried, her voice lost in the storm's roar.

"Megan, it's difficult to explain," Jack's voice carried through the tumult, its resonance cutting through the noise. "I am not Jack. I am you—or rather, who you will become."

"An ass of a pompous rich Englishman?" Megan retorted a hint of sarcasm in her tone.

Jack chuckled, the sound reverberating amidst the thunder, its force shaking the ground. "No, not quite. But there's a deeper connection between us that you can't ignore. Jack may bring you grief, but he is not inherently malevolent. He exists beyond conventional notions of good and evil. Because of this, you will want to arrest him. And despite your instincts, he is intricately tied to your future."

"No, I love Devlin!" Megan protested.

"I understand, Megan. But the connection to Jack isn't romantic. Also, unfortunately, Devlin isn't part of the path ahead for you. Trust me when I say this: Keep your eyes open, and remember, even when it feels uncertain, you can always depend on Jack."

As Jack's words hung in the air, a blinding bolt of lightning struck the ground between them, flooding Megan's vision with brilliant light. Slowly, she blinked open her eyes, greeted by the gentle morning sunlight filtering through her window. Relief washed over her as she realized she hadn't awakened screaming this time.

Epilogue

Megan stepped into the bustling office, feeling the weight of the unfinished paperwork awaiting her. The warrants for Serafim Zhukov and Kostya Alexeev hung in the air, never to be completed. They were gone, spirited away unbeknownst to anyone but Jack.

Meanwhile, the ICIS team delved into a new case, relegating their previous investigation to another department. It wasn't long until it joined the ranks of cold, forgotten mysteries archived as a cold case.

Under Jack's meticulous guidance, Gabriel established life insurance policies for Mortimer Stithulf and Abner Boone. These carefully crafted policies offered not just financial stability but also a sense of security with regular payments and educational benefits for their offspring, ensuring a future free from financial worries.

In the mayor's office, Jack awaited his scheduled appointment, his presence commanding attention amidst the flurry of activity. Donavan Layne entered the room, congratulating the grand opening's success.

"Jack, splendid to see you. Congratulations on the grand opening last night. How may I assist you today?" Donavan greeted warmly.

"Donavan, I require your assistance once more," Jack began, his voice steady and purposeful.

"Name it, and it shall be done," Donavan affirmed.

"It concerns my consultancy with the ICIS. I need to extend my involvement intermittently with team two for the foreseeable future," Jack requested.

"I'll speak with the higher-ups at ICIS. Consider it arranged," Donavan assured him.

Jack's expression turned serious as he tapped the arm of his chair. "Genbu?"

A shadow passed over Donavan's features when Jack mentioned his true identity. "Yes, Jack," he acknowledged somberly.

"It appears our next challenge may be imminent. If you receive word from the other three, inform me when the veil is on the brink of unravelling," Jack urged.

"Of course, Jack. But remember to exercise caution when using that name here. I am Donavan

Layne. We can't let others know about my true

identity from ancient times. My name back then was

lore, fairy tales of protectors and mythical beasts and

demons—fantastical, make-believe sort of things,"

Donavan reminded him.

Jack rose from his seat, adjusting his jacket

with a determined air. "I merely wished to underscore

the gravity of the situation. You personally have stood

witness many times over. Your steadfast support is

invaluable as always." With a nod of appreciation, he

retrieved his hat and cane before departing the

mayor's office.

Left alone, Donavan gazed out the window,

contemplating the looming challenges ahead. "May

this chapter be as fortuitous as the last. A good one

like you. We are counting on you, Jack," he

murmured, the weight of history heavy upon his

shoulders.

About the Author

C. T. York was born in the greater Toronto area. With a passion
for gaming and creative mediums, he pursued education in video
game design and creation. Over the years, while grappling with
deep depression and anxiety, C. T. found solace in music, using it
to fuel his days and propel him forward positively. Inspired by the
music he encountered, he began to envision characters from the
Hyde universe and develop a rich storyline. Drawing from his
own struggles, he crafted a narrative that resonates with people
from all walks of life.

Despite needing more professional writing experience, C. T.
boldly decided to pen Hyde I: Jack during personal adversity. The
challenges of the COVID-19 pandemic and the stress-induced
heart attack he experienced at a young age compelled him to
share his story. Utilizing available tools to enhance his writing, he
embarked on the creation of the first installment of a larger saga
he has been shaping for years.

****
**

I hope you enjoyed reading Hyde I: Jack, the inaugural chapter of
a tale I have been honing for quite some time. My life
experiences, coupled with my passion for music and the trials I've
faced, have fueled the creation of this story. If you found this
story engaging, spreading the word through reviews and
recommendations would greatly support the continuation of this

narrative. As I lack the means for widespread marketing, you, dear reader, serve as my marketing team. Please share this story with others if it resonates with you.

Additionally, I invite you to join my Twitch community at www.twitch.tv/wttg_ct to stay updated on future releases and our merchandise shop. Sales from this and forthcoming titles will enable me to continue creating across various mediums, with the ultimate goal of establishing my own studio to pursue my greatest passion: game development. Your participation in this journey is invaluable, and I am grateful to everyone who accompanies me.

www.ingramcontent.com/pod-product-compliance
Lightning Source LLC
Chambersburg PA
CBHW022146050726
47590CB00002B/590